Glass s

Serena's heart hammered ag
from somewhere in the house.

Josh lifted a finger to his lips, indicating silence.

She nodded and withdrew her weapon from the holster at her hip. Moving in tandem they slowly made their way down the hall toward the main part of the house. At the T in the hallway, Josh gestured with two fingers for her to go right, while he'd go left.

Hushed male voices came from the next room. At least two.

Adrenaline pumped through her veins. The nitty-gritty aspect of taking down the bad guys was a necessary part of the job. A part she had no qualms about performing.

Two men stood inside the dining room and another balanced half in, half out of the broken window on the side of the house.

Josh yelled, "Stop. U.S. Marshals."

The guy half inside the window dropped back outside and disappeared. One of the remaining thugs reached behind his back to whip out a .357 and aimed the pistol at Josh.

Fear slammed into Serena. "Gun!"

* * *

WITNESS PROTECTION: Hiding in plain sight

Books by Terri Reed

Love Inspired Suspense

*Double Deception
 Beloved Enemy
 Her Christmas Protector
*Double Jeopardy
*Double Cross
*Double Threat Christmas
 Her Last Chance
 Chasing Shadows
 Covert Pursuit
 Holiday Havoc
  "Yuletide Sanctuary"
 Daughter of Texas
†The Innocent Witness
†The Secret Heiress
 The Deputy's Duty
†The Doctor's Defender

†The Cowboy Target
 Scent of Danger
 Texas K-9 Unit Christmas
  "Rescuing Christmas"
 Treacherous Slopes
 Undercover Marriage

*The McClains
†Protection Specialists

Love Inspired

Love Comes Home
A Sheltering Love
A Sheltering Heart
A Time of Hope
Giving Thanks for Baby
Treasure Creek Dad

TERRI REED

At an early age Terri Reed discovered the wonderful world of fiction and declared she would one day write a book. Now she is fulfilling that dream and enjoys writing for Love Inspired Books. Her second book, *A Sheltering Love,* was a 2006 RITA® Award finalist and a 2005 National Readers' Choice Award finalist. Her book *Strictly Confidential,* book five in the Faith at the Crossroads continuity series, took third place in the 2007 American Christian Fiction Writers Book of the Year Award, and *Her Christmas Protector* took third place in 2008. She is an active member of both Romance Writers of America and American Christian Fiction Writers. She resides in the Pacific Northwest with her college-sweetheart husband, two wonderful children and an array of critters. When not writing, she enjoys spending time with her family and friends, gardening and playing with her dogs.

You can write to Terri at P.O. Box 19555, Portland, OR 97280. Visit her on the web at www.loveinspiredauthors.com, leave comments on her blog, www.ladiesofsuspense.blogspot.com, or email her at terrireed@sterling.net.

UNDERCOVER MARRIAGE

TERRI REED

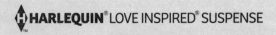

HARLEQUIN® LOVE INSPIRED® SUSPENSE

Thanks and acknowledgment to Terri Reed
for her contribution to the Witness Protection series.

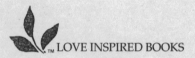

Recycling programs
for this product may
not exist in your area.

LOVE INSPIRED BOOKS

ISBN-13: 978-0-373-44600-1

UNDERCOVER MARRIAGE

I know what it is to be in need, and I know what it is to have plenty. I have learned the secret of being content in any and every situation, whether well fed or hungry, whether living in plenty or in want. I can do all this through him who gives me strength.
—*Philippians* 4:12–13

Thank you to the editors at Love Inspired for giving me this opportunity to work on this continuity series. It's been a pleasure to work with the other authors, Shirlee McCoy, Margaret Daley, Sharon Dunn, Liz Johnson and Valerie Hansen. I also want to thank Leah Vale, Lissa Manley and Melissa McClone; without their support, wisdom and laughter my life would not be as rich.

ONE

U.S. marshal Serena Summers entered three-year-old Brandon McIntyre's room with a packing box in hand. Her heart ached for the turmoil the McIntyre family had recently suffered. Danger had touched their lives in the most horrible of ways. A child had been kidnapped.

But thankfully Brandon's older brother had been rescued by the joint efforts of loving parents and the Marshals Service.

Serena paused, taking stock of the signs that the McIntyre family had once lived in this home. Little clothes spilled out of the dresser, as if the furniture had burped. Toys were scattered across the floor, tiny land mines to avoid. A toddler-size bed, the sheets and covers thrown back as if Brandon had recently awoken—and now the bed waited for the tiny body to once again claim slumber.

But the child wouldn't be back. At least not to this house.

The McIntyre family no longer lived in Houston. The U.S. Marshals Service had moved them for a second time when their location had been compromised.

Only a few people within the service knew where Dylan, Grace and the kids had been relocated.

Serena and her partner, Josh, were among them. It was their job to pack up the family's belongings and forward them through a long and winding path to their final destination. The McIntyres had been spirited away and deposited in paradise. Or as close to it as the U.S. Marshals Service could get them. Hawaii, to be exact.

Carefully picking her way around stuffed animals, train pieces and Legos, Serena went to work, gently folding clothing and stacking them inside the box. Her chest ached with empathy for the family that had almost been destroyed by the illegal activities of Dylan's boss, Fred Munders, and his thugs.

Mr. Munders, a wealthy and well-connected lawyer in St. Louis, Missouri, had been implicated in several murders and in the illegal operation of a baby-smuggling outfit run through the adoption agency his wife, Matilda Munders, founded.

The only problem was the marshals and the FBI had found no hard evidence with which to shut Munders and the adoption agency down.

The word of several thugs and Dylan McIntyre, who worked as an attorney in Munders's law firm, Munders and Moore, wasn't enough to indict. The evidence Dylan had collected against his boss had disappeared from within the Marshals Service's district offices, apparently stolen by someone within the service itself.

Serena's fingers curled with anger around the tiny tennis shoe in her hand.

So many deaths, so many lives thrown into chaos.

The thought that someone she worked with, trusted, could have stolen the evidence and could have been leaking information to the bad guys sent Serena's blood to boil.

If her brother were alive, he'd know how to compartmentalize the anger and pain gnawing at her day in and day out.

But Daniel was gone. Murdered.

A sharp stab of grief sliced through her heart. Followed closely by the anger that always chased her sorrow.

She tossed the shoe in the box and abruptly rose. Restless, she moved to strip the bed. She had to keep busy, keep her mind occupied, or her emotions would overwhelm her. Something she refused to let happen. She needed to stay professional. She needed to keep up the front that her world hadn't collapsed with her brother's death.

"Hey, you okay in here?"

Serena glanced up at her current partner, U.S. marshal Josh McCall. They'd been paired to work the illegal adoption case. His six-foot-three frame filled the doorway. He'd taken off his navy suit jacket and rolled the sleeves of his once crisp white dress shirt up to the elbows. His silver silk tie was askew, and his brown hair looked as if he'd been running his fingers through it again, the ends standing up, making him appear as if he'd just rolled out of bed rather than put in a ninety-hour week. His soft brown eyes, shadowed by signs of fatigue and grief, tugged at her heart. She'd always found him appealing. But that was before. Now she refused to allow her reaction to show. Not only did she not want to draw attention to the fact that she'd noticed anything about him, she didn't want him to think she cared.

She didn't. Josh was the reason her brother had been alone when he'd been murdered. Instead of having his partner's back, Josh had been out on a personal day at the time Daniel needed him, leaving Daniel on his own to chase a lead, where he was struck on the head and left to die. Alone.

A traitorous thought niggled: Daniel shouldn't have gone off by himself. Doing so went against protocol and logic. If he hadn't, he would still be alive. She pushed back her musings. Her brother must have had a good reason. But nothing absolved Josh of the responsibility he had to protect Daniel. They'd been best friends as well as coworkers.

Her fists bunched up the bedding. Her soul cried out with "Why, Lord?" as it always did anytime she allowed her mind to go down that road.

Turning away from Josh, she said briskly, "I'm good."

Taking the two ends of the sheet in each hand, she spread her arms wide and attempted to fold the sheet in half. The material didn't want to cooperate.

"Here," Josh said, stepping all the way into the room. "Let me help."

He reached for the sheet, his hand brushing hers.

An electric current shot through her. She jerked away, letting go of the ends as if she'd been burned. The sheet fluttered to the floor between them. "I don't need your help."

His hand dropped to his side. "Serena." Josh's tone held a note of hurt.

Inhaling sharply, Serena berated herself for not being professional. She'd allowed her personal grief and bitterness to show. She stiffened her spine, raised her chin and let out a long breath.

Keeping her voice neutral, she asked, "How's the kitchen coming along?"

Resignation shuttered his expression. "Almost done."

"Good. I finished the kids' bathroom and the daughter's room. Those boxes are ready for transport."

"We'll be out of here in time to make our scheduled flight," Josh stated, his tone flat. "It'll be good to return to St. Louis and get some rest."

Serena's mouth pressed tight. Rest was something she'd had little of the past year and a half, ever since her brother's unsolved murder. Not to mention the trips to various locations around the country as she and Josh worked to track down leads on the illegal baby-smuggling scheme. Each lead only brought more confusion and chaos. They badly needed a break in the case.

Glass shattered.

Serena's heart hammered against her ribs.

The sound came from somewhere in the house.

Josh raised a finger to his lips, indicating silence.

She nodded and withdrew her weapon from the holster at her hip. Moving in tandem, they slowly made their way down the hall toward the main part of the house. At the T in the hallway, Josh gestured with two fingers for her to go right, while he'd go left.

Dipping her chin in acknowledgment, she peeled off to enter the empty kitchen. Her pulse beat a frantic tempo.

Hushed male voices came from the next room. At least two.

The muscles in her shoulders tightened. Adrenaline pumped through her veins. The nitty-gritty aspect of taking down the bad guys was a necessary part of the job. A part she had no qualms about performing. As a woman in a field historically dominated by men, she'd worked hard to prove herself. Just as other women in the service had done as far back as the late 1800s, when Ada Carnutt first put on the badge. Serena admired her predecessors as well as the current female director of the U.S. Marshals Service, who'd been appointed by the president. Serena would do them proud.

Skirting around stacked boxes, she made her way to the dining room just as Josh entered from the living room.

Two men stood inside the dining room and another was balanced half in, half out of the broken window on the side of the house. All three men, dressed in black, were big guys in their late twenties.

Josh yelled, "Stop! U.S. Marshals!"

The guy half inside the window dropped back outside and disappeared. One of the remaining thugs reached behind his back to whip out a .357 and aimed the pistol at Josh.

Fear burst within Serena. "Gun!"

Josh ducked behind a stack of boxes as the guy holding the gun fired in his direction. A bullet tore through the cardboard box, nearly taking out Josh's eye, and smashed into the wall. She dove behind the love seat.

Knowing the boxes wouldn't provide enough cover for Josh, Serena had to do something. She popped up, aimed at the intruder with the gun and squeezed off a round. The rapid beat of her heart thundered in her ears, drowning out the retort of the weapon in her hand. The bullet slammed into the guy's leg. He screamed and crumpled to the floor. His buddy jumped through the broken window and escaped.

Serena leaped to her feet and raced around the love seat, keeping her weapon trained on the man writhing on the floor, clutching his leg. She kicked aside the gun he'd dropped.

"You okay?" Josh asked as he skidded to a halt beside her.

She nodded, her gaze searching him for injury.

"Good." He rushed toward the window. "Watch him. I'm going after the other two."

Chest knotting, Serena watched Josh disappear through the window.

"Keep him safe, Lord," she whispered and hoped God would listen. She blamed Josh for her brother's death, but she didn't want to have to live through another loss. She'd known Josh a long time. He and Daniel had been friends since basic training at the academy in Glynco, Georgia, over eight years ago.

She dug her cell phone out of the pocket of her suit jacket and called the Houston district office and the police department for backup. While she waited, she cuffed the guy's hands in front of him and then grabbed a towel from a box to press against the bullet wound.

The man moaned. "You shot me."

She refrained from pointing out he'd shot first. "Who sent you?"

"I don't know," the guy ground out. "I need a doctor!"

"What were you doing here?" Serena asked.

"Trying to find out where they went."

Serena didn't need to ask who; she knew he meant Dylan and his family. "What were you supposed to do with the information?"

"I don't know. Bob set this up. He'd know."

"Bob who? What's Bob's last name?"

The guy clamped his mouth shut.

"Come on, give me the name. It will go better for you if you do," Serena coaxed.

"I want a lawyer." A spasm of pain marched across his face. "I'm not saying anything more."

Serena blew out a frustrated breath.

The wail of a siren announced the arrival of the Houston police force. Josh reentered the house through the front door, leading paramedics and two police officers inside.

Serena relinquished her hold on the rag to the paramedics and joined Josh off to the side so the local LEOs—law enforcement officers—could take over.

"Mr. Bad Shot said they were looking to find out where Dylan and the family went," she told Josh. "Said one of his buddies named Bob set up the deal."

"Good job getting that out of him."

The approval in Josh's brown eyes made her stand a little taller. She still only reached his shoulder. "I take it the other two got away?"

"Yeah, they had a vehicle on the next block. I got a partial plate."

"We have to put a stop to this," Serena said. "We have to bring Munders down once and for all!"

Josh swiped a hand through his hair. "We will. First things first. Let's finish up here and get home to St. Louis."

Home. The word reverberated through Serena's head like a pinball, bouncing off her thoughts. Growing up, she and Daniel had been passed around between their divorced parents like a set of candlesticks that neither really wanted but didn't want the other to have. When Daniel had reached the age of majority he'd moved out on his own, taking Serena with him.

They'd shared an apartment ever since, but after Daniel's death, she couldn't take being there without him. She'd given everything to a local charity and moved into a studio. Her apartment wasn't a home. It was a place to store her stuff and to sleep when she could.

She didn't know if she'd ever have a real home again. Without her brother in her life, she was lost. He'd been her anchor. The one constant. Home had been where he was. Now he was gone. Thanks to Josh.

"Will we make our flight?" Serena asked, as the moving van, escorted by Houston police, pulled away from the curb.

Josh checked the time on his smartphone. "With time to spare."

With the help of two local marshals, they'd made short work of packing the last of the McIntyre household into boxes and loading them onto the transport bound for Hawaii via Chicago and Seattle.

The Houston marshals had taken the wounded thug into custody and had obtained Josh's and Serena's statements. Josh wished they'd had another chance to further interrogate the guy who'd broken into the McIntyre house, but he didn't want to get into an arm-wrestling match for control of the situation.

He'd let his superiors deal with the politics. Local marshals would interrogate the man later. And hopefully he would give up information on his cohorts.

After locking up the house, Serena placed the key in the mail slot for the landlord. The small circle of light from the porch fixture didn't extend to the driveway, where they had parked the green four-door sedan they'd rented when they arrived in Houston this morning. Darkness shrouded the driveway and the bushes on either side.

The need for caution tripped down Josh's spine.

He placed a hand to the small of Serena's back. The fabric of her pantsuit felt luxurious against his palm.

She stiffened at his touch and stepped away.

Ignoring the sliver of irritation that sliced through him, he opened the passenger door and she slid into the seat. He reached inside to help untangle the seat belt strap. She shifted away from him and wouldn't meet his gaze.

He blew out a frustrated breath and finished righting the belt before backing away and slamming the door shut.

They were both tired and cranky.

At least that was how he explained away her reaction every time he got close to her. But then again, these days she was always prickly with him.

Besides the one glimpse of vulnerability on her face when she'd been packing young Brandon's room, Serena was her stoic self. Saying little and showing even less in her expression. The professional to the nth degree.

Her lack of emotions set his nerves on edge.

He wished she'd get mad or sad or something. She was grieving for Daniel, yet she held on to her emotions with an iron fist. He tried to emulate her. But it took a lot of energy to repress the myriad emotions raging through him at any given moment. There were times he wanted to give up, but knowing he had to stay focused and in the game for Serena's sake kept him going.

He missed the easy friendship he and Serena had had before Daniel's death. But since the moment she'd heard of her brother's murder, she'd retreated behind this ascetic silence, talking to him only when necessary.

Not easy when they had to work together.

Sometimes impossible as partners assigned to a tough case.

He blew out a puff of air.

He knew she hadn't been happy to be paired with him. But they made a good team regardless of their personal issues. Each easily anticipated the other's need, the other's movements. Numerous colleagues had commented on their compatibility. In fact, many people thought they were so in sync with each other that they could be a romantic couple.

So not the case.

For so many reasons.

First and foremost, Serena was Daniel's sister and therefore off-limits. There were few people in this world Josh trusted. Daniel had been at the top of the list. Dishonoring his memory by becoming romantically involved with his sister wasn't something he intended to do.

Besides, Josh would never do anything to jeopardize his working relationship with Serena by pursuing her romantically.

Josh had tried on numerous occasions over the past year and a half to talk to Serena about the day Daniel died, but she'd refused to engage in a conversation. Not that he wanted to explain why he'd taken a personal day or why he hadn't answered the phone when Daniel had called him hours before his death.

What he wanted to tell Serena was how gut-wrenching

it had been to learn of Daniel's murder and then hearing Daniel's voice message asking for backup.

Josh would live with the knowledge he'd let his fellow marshal and best friend down because of a woman. Lexi, Josh's girlfriend of three years, had dumped him that morning, accusing him of having feelings for Serena.

Not putting any stock in the accusation, he'd dismissed Lexi's allegations as irrational jealousy. Lexi had always been territorial, but she'd gone too far this time.

Josh wouldn't deny he found Serena attractive, with her long dark hair captured back into a low ponytail and her wide-set eyes that saw through him. The tailored pantsuits she wore covered her from head to toe but showed off her athletic and feminine curves underneath. When Josh had first met Serena, she'd been reserved and wary, but she had warmed up over the years that Daniel had been Josh's friend.

Josh wouldn't have felt right about pursuing Serena, especially after she started working alongside him and Daniel. Josh had forced his attraction into a box and made himself treat Serena like a little sister when they weren't working and like a professional colleague when they were.

None of that mattered now. Daniel was gone. Serena was now virtually a stranger, and Josh had no intention of becoming romantically involved with her. His guilt wouldn't let him. He didn't deserve happiness or even contentment.

He was to blame for Daniel's death.

He would never forgive himself.

With a heavy heart, he drove out of the neighborhood and merged onto the highway heading toward Houston's Intercontinental Airport. The evening traffic had thinned.

He glanced in the rearview mirror, noting the headlights of a black SUV. The same vehicle had been behind them since they left the suburban neighborhood. The big black beast stayed two cars back. Josh moved into the right lane to see what the SUV would do. It changed lanes, as well. At the last second Josh took the off-ramp.

"Hey!" Serena cried, reaching up for the grab-handle.

The SUV shot down the ramp behind them.

"We're being followed," Josh stated.

Serena swiveled in her seat to look out the back window. "I can't make out the license plate."

Josh stepped on the gas, heading the sedan down a side street. The back window exploded as gunfire pebbled the car.

Up ahead an empty parking lot came into view. Josh made a sharp turn into the parking lot. Then, keeping his foot on the gas, he twisted the steering wheel, sending the sedan into a ninety-degree spin. When the front end faced the oncoming SUV, he stomped on the brake and threw the gear shift into Park.

Popping open the driver's-side door with one hand, he yanked his Sig Sauer out of its holster beneath his jacket. Beside him Serena did the same with her Walther. Using the door as a shield, he aimed at the oncoming vehicle.

Blinding light from the high beams made him wince. He fired off a shot, taking out one headlight.

Undeterred, the SUV barreled toward them.

Panic cramped Josh's chest.

The crazy driver wasn't going to stop.

TWO

"Look out!" Serena cried, as the SUV headed for a collision course with the sedan.

Her heart crawled into her throat and constricted her breathing. Galvanized by self-preservation, she scrambled away from the open passenger door. Anticipation of the SUV crashing into Josh's sedan stiffened every muscle in her body. She braced herself for the impact and glanced back. Josh hadn't moved!

"Josh!" Why wasn't he getting out of the way? "Move it. Now!"

He squeezed off several rounds, hitting the front of the SUV.

At the last second the SUV veered to the left, roaring past the driver's side of the sedan. The barrel of an assault rifle stuck out the open back passenger window.

A barrage of gunfire split the air. Bullets riddled the fender and door of the rental sedan. The deafening noise echoed inside Serena's head.

Josh dove inside the car.

Serena rolled to her knees, aimed and fired, hitting the back window. The SUV screamed out of the parking lot and disappeared down the street.

Heavy silence descended.

Fear for Josh overwhelmed Serena. *Please, dear Lord, don't let him be dead.*

She jumped to her feet and rushed to the car. "Josh! Are you hurt?"

Josh jolted to a seated position to pound his palm against the steering wheel, his frustration obvious. He yanked out his cell and called 911.

She sagged forward with relief that he was okay and braced a hand on the car roof. Losing her brother had sent her into an emotional tailspin that she'd barely begun to come out of. Losing a partner wasn't something she wanted to go through, no matter what her personal feelings for said partner were.

Taking a deep breath, she grabbed the edges of her professionalism and pulled it tightly around her before stepping back to allow Josh to climb out of the car.

"Did you happen to see the shooters?" he asked.

"No, the windows were tinted. Do you think they were the same perps from the house?"

"Pretty likely that it was. We saw their faces." His usually warm brown eyes hardened. "I'm sure they figured if they got rid of us then there'd be no one to ID them."

"Except the guy I shot could identify them," Serena said. "We need to let the local marshals know they might have a potential target on their hands."

"Good idea." He loosened his tie then swiped a hand down his face.

A smear of blood on the back of his hand caught her attention. "You're hurt."

He glanced down at the cut where flying glass had scraped across his skin. "Hazard of the job."

Right. She knew all too well the dangers that came with being a U.S. marshal. Her brother died in the line of duty. Would she and Josh suffer the same fate?

* * *

The next morning Josh rolled into work five minutes before eight. A sleek skyscraper in downtown St. Louis housed the U.S. Marshals Service district office. Josh took the elevator to the fourth floor and made his way to his desk. Serena was already seated at her station a few feet away. She glanced up, gave him a tight smile and returned her focus to the file in front of her.

In contrast to her neat and tidy desk, Josh's desk had a mound of files stacked precariously close to the edge. A desktop weekly planner, sporting coffee stains, still showed the previous month. He took a seat and ripped the top sheet off the calendar so that June would show. He powered up his laptop.

"Hey, McCall." Marshal Burke Trier stopped beside Josh's desk. Tall and lean with dark eyes, dark hair and a dimpled chin, Burke was the resident ladies' man. "Glad to see you made it back in one piece. We heard about the ambush last night."

"News travels fast," Josh remarked. "What's happening with the Munders case?"

Burke shrugged. "We're stalled out. Without the evidence McIntyre promised we're going nowhere real fast."

"Not his fault the thumb drive containing the evidence went missing while in our custody," Josh shot back.

"Yeah, well, if there was anything on it to begin with," Burke stated. "Maybe McIntyre lifted it while we had our backs turned."

Josh's fingers curled. "Dylan McIntyre was trying to do the right thing. He wouldn't—"

"Any leads on the missing Baby Kay or her mother?" Serena interjected. "That's what we need to keep focused on."

Josh's gut twisted. Leave it to Serena to use the one thing that would defuse the situation. A few months back a woman named Emma Bullock had been found beaten and unconscious in Minneapolis. When she awoke, she couldn't remember who she was or who'd hurt her. However, she remembered being in possession of a baby at the time of the attack. But the baby was nowhere to be found.

Apparently a young woman named Lonnie had asked Emma to safeguard her child while she ran an errand but had never returned. The marshals were called in because of the illegal adoption ring they were on the cusp of busting. Josh was sure the kidnapping of Baby Kay had something to do with Munders and the Perfect Family Adoption Agency. The police and the Marshals Service were still searching for the baby and the young mother.

Burke shook his head. "Unfortunately, no. The Minneapolis P.D. is staying on top of the search and will keep us informed if anything develops."

Josh let out a frustrated grunt for a reply. He prayed the young mother and baby were still alive.

"Burke, what do you hear from Hunter?" Serena asked. She rested her elbows on the desktop and steepled her hands as she waited for an answer.

Hunter Davis had been their team leader until he'd taken an extended leave of absence. He'd fallen in love with a witness he'd been protecting. But he was still consulting on the baby-smuggling case via telephone from time to time.

"He and Annie got married. Didn't invite any of us." The disgruntled note in Burke's voice was understandable. He and Hunter had been roommates before Hunter met Annie. She'd entered the witness protection program to testify against the men who'd killed her husband and tried to kidnap her daughter.

"Good for them," Serena said.

Josh stared at her. Had he just seen a flash of longing? She met his gaze and immediately her dark brown eyes

cooled before she turned her attention to the file in front
of her. Nah. He'd been dreaming. The only thing in her
eyes was pure steel.

"Good morning, children." A booming voice echoed
through the offices as recently retired U.S. marshal Bud
Hollingsworth approached, bearing a box of treats from
a local bakery. Tall with a potbelly, the sixty-something
veteran was having a hard time adjusting to retirement, if
his frequent appearances at the office were any indication.
"I understand you two had some trouble over in Houston."

"Does everyone know?" Josh asked. "How did you
hear?"

Bud shrugged and lifted the lid on the box to offer Josh
a pastry. "The chief. He asked me to come in and consult
on this development. I'm going to liaison with the Houston P.D. to try to catch these guys. We can't have our witness compromised."

Josh's defenses rose. "He wasn't. There were no labels
on anything. No way anyone could find out where the
McIntyre family has been relocated to."

"Josh. Serena," Chief U.S. Marshal Wendell Harrison
called from the doorway of his office. In his fifties, lean
and wiry, Wendell exuded energy without trying. "A word,
please."

Exchanging a curious glance with Serena, Josh pushed
out of his chair and stood. He followed Serena into the
chief's office. The chief sat behind his desk. Another man
wearing a gray pin-striped suit rose as they entered. About
five foot five, muscular, with a chiseled jaw and swept-
back blond hair, the man oozed fed.

"Marshal McCall and Marshal Summers, you know
FBI Special Agent Todd Bishop," Harrison said.

Bishop shook Josh's hand, then Serena's. "Marshals,"
Bishop said. "You two have been doing good work."

"Thank you," Serena said, looking pleased. She was

a woman who liked to be praised for her work. Compliments about anything else were met with a silent stare.

Without preamble, the chief said in a loud booming voice, "In light of last night's development and close call, I'm taking you two off the Munders case and reassigning you to a new case. We'll be coordinating with Agent Bishop."

The air rushed from Josh's lungs as if he'd been socked in the stomach. Six months ago when he and Serena had been assigned to this special operation, he'd welcomed the chance to coordinate with the FBI in tracking down and apprehending criminals connected to the illegal adoption ring.

Anything to distract himself from the anguish of his best friend's murder. Though investigating wasn't within the scope of the Marshals Service, Josh had done what he could to find Daniel's killer as well as monitored the local police and federal investigation, but they, too, had hit dead ends at every turn.

Now to be taken off the special operation they'd toiled at for so many months chafed.

"What? No." Serena's protest drew the attention of everyone in the outer offices. "We've worked too hard on this case to be taken off now."

Harrison held up a hand. "Please. I understand you're upset. But this is for your protection."

Josh tucked in his chin. "Our protection? We're doing fine. We have each other's back."

Harrison regarded them steadily with steely blue eyes. "Shut the door and take a seat."

Serena pushed the door closed. "I'd rather stand."

Josh took the seat opposite his boss. Special Agent Bishop moved to hitch a hip onto the edge of the desk.

The chief's expression was grim, but there was something else in his assessing eyes that made Josh guess there was more to this. "Sir? What's *really* going on?"

Harrison's mouth twitched. "You are a perceptive man, McCall."

"I try, sir."

"Serena, close the blinds, please," Harrison instructed.

Once the blinds were closed, Serena stood behind the empty chair next to Josh, her hands gripping the back.

Harrison leaned forward. "I'm not taking you off the Munders case," he said, his voice low, intense. "That bit was for show. I don't want whoever our leak is to know what you're actually going to be doing."

"Which is?" Josh prompted, anxious.

"You're going undercover," Agent Bishop stated.

Surprise washed through Josh. "Isn't that something the FBI should be doing?" A few months ago, FBI agent Lisette Sutton had gone undercover in a fertility clinic. The Marshals Service had provided support in the form of U.S. marshal Colton Phillips.

"Normally, yes," Bishop said. "But these are special circumstances that will require you to wear the mantle of investigator. We have every confidence in the two of you."

Josh wasn't sure he shared Bishop's certainty. They hadn't been successful yet in plugging the department leak or apprehending the man known as "Mr. Big."

"We need hard evidence against Munders and the Perfect Family Adoption Agency to take to the state attorney general," the chief said. "I want you two to get it."

"Where are we going undercover and as what?" Serena asked in a tone mixed with equal parts excitement and apprehension. Josh felt that same mix in his gut. He waited for the chief's answer.

Harrison sat back. "Before I go into the details, bring Agent Bishop up to speed on where we are in the investigation."

"I've read the reports, but I'd like to hear your observations," Agent Bishop said.

Josh looked to Serena. Her gaze slid to meet his. Her eyebrows inched up in question. Josh nodded, indicating for her to speak.

"Six months ago a routine court witness protection detail went south," she said, addressing Agent Bishop. "We apprehended a suspect who had tried to take out the witness and offered him protection in exchange for information regarding human trafficking. Babies, to be exact. The thug was working for someone dubbed 'Mr. Big.' We have yet to find this man.

"However, following the lead the suspect provided, we ascertained that there is indeed an illegal ring of baby smugglers operating out of the U.S. We believe the headquarters are here in St. Louis. We discovered a connection between Mexico and a law firm here, Munders and Moore.

"We believe the law firm is arranging for infants to be brought across the border and sold to American families through an adoption agency."

"The Perfect Family Adoption Agency," Harrison murmured. "Why there?"

"The agency is owned and operated by Matilda Munders, wife of Fred Munders. Fred has been implicated in witness tampering, several kidnappings and murder."

The chief stroked his chin. "It's imperative we bring these criminals to justice. Are you two prepared to do what it takes?"

Josh blinked at the ominous words. He glanced at Special Agent Bishop. The man stared back at him with sharp eyes, reminding Josh of a shark.

"Yes, sir," Serena answered quickly.

"Josh?" Harrison eyed him with an intensity that made Josh want to squirm.

But Josh held himself still. "Of course, sir."

"Good." Agent Bishop handed each of them a file folder. "Inside this dossier you will find everything you need for your cover. Publically you will be reassigned to work on a fugitive task force coordinating with the FBI."

Josh opened the dossier and scanned the overview sheet. His heart beat in his throat. He slanted a glance at Serena. She stood frozen in place, her gaze trained on the papers in her hand. Slowly she lifted her gaze to meet his. Shock and denial swirled in the depths of her chocolate-brown eyes.

Swiftly she jerked her gaze away from Josh to address the chief. "No. I can't. I won't."

Josh's fingers tightened around the folder. He'd never known Serena to back away from a challenge. And this would be challenging.

The chief stared back at her unflinchingly. "This is too dangerous a task to give to a civilian. You and McCall are the perfect choices."

She sputtered. "But…but…posing as husband and wife?"

"It's the perfect cover," Bishop said. "You'll be Mr. and Mrs. Andrews from Alaska, recently relocated to St. Louis because of Mr. Andrews's promotion to bank executive at First National. You are desperate to have a child. You've tried everything and are at your wits' end."

"I could never pull this off," Serena declared, her voice rising slightly, betraying her upset.

Josh had only seen her lose her cool once, when she'd heard the news of her brother's death. For her to show this much of a reaction spoke volumes. Was it the undercover work she objected to, or was it that he would be playing her husband?

"Serena, think of all the innocent families who have been affected by this case." Josh held her gaze. He needed to take this assignment. *They* needed to take this assignment. They'd worked too hard over the past six months to back down now.

The fact that going undercover with Serena would mean they'd be in constant contact with few breaks strung his nerves tight, but he couldn't let that deter him. "We need to do this. We need to bring the ringleaders to justice before more hearts are broken—or anyone else is killed."

A ripple of pain crossed Serena's face before she narrowed her gaze on him. "You're okay with this? You and me posing as husband and wife?"

"If that is what is required of us, then yes. I would think you'd want to do whatever it took to bring down Munders and the adoption agency. Even posing as my wife."

The thought of pretending to be married to Serena—aka Susan Andrews—would present all sorts of difficulties. Not the least of which was the attraction he fought on a daily basis, and despite the fact that they had reached an uneasy truce these past few months, he could never forget that she blamed him for Daniel's death. Nor could he ignore his own guilt, which made working with Serena so painful.

Playing the part of Jack Andrews would necessitate Josh's tapping into his latent acting skills. In high school he'd had the lead role of Algernon Moncrieff in *The Importance of Being Earnest,* to much acclaim.

Though a part of him doubted he'd have much trouble giving a convincing act as "Susan's" husband. Not with Serena playing Susan to his Jack.

But the question that knocked at his mind was: once this charade was finished, would they be able to go back to being partners?

Serena barely held on to her composure as three sets of eyes watched her. She forced her expression to remain neutral. She hated that she'd had a momentary lapse in poise when she initially realized what they were being asked to do.

Pose as husband and wife?

Her and Josh.

A loving couple wanting to adopt a child.

The thought of pretending to be Josh's adoring wife sent her heart rate spiking and stirred up old feelings she'd long ago squashed. When she'd first met her brother's friend, she thought Josh handsome and charming. It didn't hurt that Daniel had loved Josh like a brother. But Josh had been taken. And Serena had a strict policy to never poach another woman's man. Not that she had wanted to date Josh. Well, okay, maybe a little, even though he'd treated her like a sister and kept a proper distance between them. She'd admired his faithfulness to his girlfriend. There had been a lot about Josh Serena had admired and respected.

But that was before Daniel's murder.

Now she tolerated Josh's presence because she had to, not because she held on to some silly crush.

She dropped her gaze to the file in her hand. The dossier held a minimal biography of the fictional Susan Andrews as well as a birth certificate and a social security number. Both documents looked completely legit. Everything she'd need for a Missouri ID.

Even though this identity was temporary and would be used only for the purpose of bringing down criminals, a surreal feeling of loss of self invaded her.

This must be what witnesses felt when they were given their new identities.

The silence stretched as the men waited for her to say something. She thought about the children who'd been torn away from their mothers and sold off to couples desperate enough to purchase a baby through questionable sources.

Those little lives demanded she put aside her personal

issues and do what was necessary to make sure no more families were torn apart.

"I'm in." She slanted a glance to her "husband," then quickly jerked her gaze away when her heart jumped.

She'd better learn to compartmentalize ASAP or their cover would be blown before it ever got off the ground.

THREE

"Excellent." Agent Bishop glanced at Chief Harrison and exchanged a nod. Josh tugged at the collar of his shirt. "Welcome to Operation: Marriage."

"Uh, don't you mean Operation: Undercover Marriage?" Josh asked, earning himself one of Serena's annoyed, you-think-you're-so-funny looks.

Bishop chuckled. "Right you are, Marshal McCall." He clasped Josh's hand in a firm grip. "Glad to have you on board." He released Josh to take Serena's hand. "I'm looking forward to working with you."

Bishop held on a little too long to Serena's hand. Josh's gaze narrowed. The soft smile she gave the agent pierced Josh with a spear of jealousy that both shocked and scared him. Daniel had made Josh promise that if anything ever happened to him, Josh would watch out for Serena. No way should he be feeling anything like jealousy—or anything else, for that matter—toward his partner.

Wife.

Pretend wife.

Daniel's sister!

Get a grip, McCall. This was just his job. A part to be played for the sake of a lot of kids' safety, on behalf of justice. Nothing more.

Giving himself a mental shake, he turned to the chief. "When do we start this charade?"

"Immediately," the chief answered.

"I'll have a house set up for you within the hour," Bishop said.

"Where will the house be located?" Serena asked. "If we're posing as a wealthy couple looking to adopt a child at any price, we're going to need to be set up in one of the more affluent neighborhoods."

"On it," Bishop said. "I have an agent securing a home in the Compton Heights neighborhood. You will also need a high-end vehicle appropriate for your cover as a bank executive. Stop by the BMW dealership on South Hanley Road. Ask for Dirk. He's expecting you."

Josh whistled between his teeth. "Wow, we'll get to see how the other half lives."

A car and a home in Compton Heights. The posh neighborhood was located on the near south side of the city in the shadow of the great water tower of Reservoir Park. The nationally historic neighborhood sported gated and tree-lined streets and houses that were mostly of the Victorian era with lavish yards.

A world unto itself with the convenience of being ten minutes from everywhere. A lifestyle Josh would never be able to afford on a marshal's salary. But he didn't regret the choice he made to join the U.S. Marshals Service. He wouldn't allow money to hold the same appeal to him as it had to his father. Josh had strived too hard in the course of his life to be the opposite of the man who'd broken not only his mother's heart but also Josh's.

"Will we have operational support?" Serena asked.

"You will," the chief stated. "You both remember Linda Maitland?"

Serena shook her head. "I don't."

"I do." Josh remembered Linda well. She'd served as

the administrative officer when he'd joined the St. Louis district office. She'd retired not long after.

"She'll be coming on board as your support. Her cover will be an aunt who's living with you." Harrison exchanged a glance with Bishop. "We wanted someone we were sure wasn't the leak but who would be familiar with our protocols."

"There will also be an agent posing as the grounds-keeper to provide additional support," Bishop said. His pocket beeped. He withdrew a cell phone. "Excuse me." He moved to the corner of the room and stood with his back to them while he took his call.

"Will we be able to pack clothing from home?" Serena asked.

Harrison regarded her kindly. "As Mrs. Andrews, you'll be expected to dress the part."

Serena blinked. "I better go shopping."

"Turn your receipts in to Linda and she'll make sure you're reimbursed." Harrison turned to Josh. "Your suits should be fine, though you should try to change your appearance as much as you can. You'll need to leave each morning like you're going to work. Agent Bishop will arrange for an office in the bank headquarters on the executive floor where you can continue with your investigation into Munders and the adoption agency."

Serena frowned. "What about me?"

"You'll be the devoted stay-at-home wife waiting to adopt a child," Harrison explained. "You will definitely need to change your appearance. Work with Linda on that."

Serena's mouth pressed tight. She didn't like the idea, which didn't surprise Josh. She wasn't the stay-at-home type. She was one of the most ambitious women he knew. A trait that would take her far. Her work ethic was one of the qualities that he admired about her.

Bishop clicked off his call and rejoined them. "Actually, Marshal Summers, there is a family in the neighborhood with several adopted children. We don't know if they've dealt with Perfect Family or not. We'd like you to establish a connection."

"Okay, I can do that," Serena said with certainty ringing in her tone.

This Josh had to see. Serena's no-nonsense, practical and professional demeanor worked in the field, but would it work in an affluent suburban neighborhood?

"Good. That call was from my agent in the field. The house is ready." Bishop wrote an address on a sheet of paper and handed it to Josh. "Ms. Maitland will meet you there." He handed them each a business card. "If you need anything, my numbers are on here." He shook hands with the chief before exiting out the door.

"Okay," the chief said. "You have your marching orders. Do us proud and get the goods on Munders."

"We will, sir," Josh assured him and filed out of the chief's office behind Serena.

Burke Trier was the first to pounce with curiosity. "So what was that about?"

"Are you two really being pulled off the Munders case?" Bud Hollingsworth asked. "That doesn't make sense. You two have been the one constant."

"Yep, we're pulled," Serena stated with an exaggerated sigh. "It's not fair. We've worked so hard to be taken out now."

Burke gave her a funny look.

Josh stifled a groan. If this overdone display was any indication of Serena's acting abilities, they were in trouble.

"We're being reassigned to a FBI task force here in town," Josh said, offering the cover story.

"For what?" Bud asked.

Josh shrugged. "Don't know yet. We're leaving now."

Bud clapped him on the back. "Tough break. That must be why Harrison called me in."

"Must be." Josh gathered his things. "You ready, partner?"

Serena met his gaze. "Yes, partner."

They left the building. In the parking garage, they decided to take Josh's sedan and leave Serena's compact. Driving through downtown St. Louis traffic, Josh said, "We should discuss the Andrewses' backstory. Where we met. Why we can't have children. What lengths we'd go to for a child."

Serena slanted him a glance. "According to this, we met in college."

"Okay. Where?"

She opened the file folder. "This says you're transferring to St. Louis from Alaska." She wrinkled her nose. "I can't imagine living in Alaska. But first we met in Seattle at the University of Washington. You went to work for the bank right out of college and then we were moved to Alaska and now St. Louis."

"Okay. Once we get settled in the house, we contact the adoption agency and tell them we want a child right away." Josh drummed his fingers on the steering wheel. "What kind of person adopts a baby who seemingly appears overnight?"

"Desperate ones," Serena said.

"If people want to adopt, they should use a reputable and legal agency that is regulated by the state they live in."

"I would imagine the families that have adopted through Perfect Family Adoption Agency thought it was a legitimate agency. If the Munderses weren't so good at hiding the illegal aspects of their agency, we'd have shut them down long before now," she reminded him.

"True. But I still don't get why anyone would not be suspicious if a baby was produced quickly without meeting the birth mother. Someone can't just show up to an adoption agency and expect to have an infant in their arms within a short amount of time. We already know that Munders's organization, working in Mexico, coerced Vanessa Martinez into giving up her baby, Isabella."

Four months ago U.S. marshal Colton Phillips had been assigned to protect the thug who'd promised information on the illegal baby-buying scheme. In the process, Colton and FBI agent Lisette Sutton had stopped the illegal transfer of a baby they dubbed Baby C. The infant was eventually reunited with her mother. A win for the marshals.

"It's not our place to judge what others do. People have to walk their own paths."

"That's very magnanimous of you," he stated, a bit surprised by her soft attitude. It made him wonder what lay beneath the tough exterior she so valiantly exuded.

She shrugged. "If a couple had tried everything to have their own child and then were forced to wait months and months or even years to adopt through the state-run agencies, I could see how they'd turn to agencies that might be a bit questionable."

"It sounds like you've given the subject some thought." Did she long for a child of her own? Her unrelenting professionalism made him wonder what type of mother she'd be.

What type of wife?

The fact that he wanted to find out made him shift uncomfortably in his seat. He had no business letting his mind wander down such a dangerous path.

"Don't be ridiculous," she snapped. "I'm just hypothesizing."

"No maternal pangs?"

From the corner of his eye he saw her jaw clench.

There was a moment of hesitation before she said, "No.

But I do know what it's like to desperately wish for something that you can't have."

She wasn't referring to children or the case but rather to her wish that Daniel were still alive. He had the same desperate, useless desire. But Daniel was gone. His absence left a gaping hole in Josh's life. The hole was even bigger in Serena's life.

"Daniel would like this undercover idea," Josh stated softly.

"Yes, he'd have relished playing the role of wealthy Jack Andrews," Serena replied and turned to look out the passenger window.

Josh gave a quiet laugh. "Yeah, but I'd never be able to pull off the doting wife bit. My ankles give me away every time."

She shook her head, but he saw the slight smile. A part of her clearly appreciated his attempt at levity, but she was obviously still too raw, still hurting from the loss of her brother, to laugh too much.

His chest caved in on itself under the heavy weight of guilt.

He pulled up outside his apartment building. "I know this charade of pretending to be my wife is going to be hard for you, Serena."

She jerked her gaze to him. "What's that supposed to mean?"

"As professionals we need to put our personal feelings aside. Daniel wouldn't want to be the reason we didn't crack this case."

Her brown eyes hardened. "I'll do *my* job, Josh."

The tone of her voice suggested that he wouldn't do his. He bristled with offense. Old fears that he'd be like his father rose to taunt him. "Are you questioning my work ethic?"

"You weren't there for Daniel when he needed you."

Josh flinched; her words were a blow to the gut. He knew she blamed him for Daniel's death. Having that bit of gut-clenching knowledge confirmed tore a jagged hole through him. "I had taken a personal day. Daniel understood."

"But he called you right before he—" Her voice caught. "And yet you weren't there for him."

Josh's heart contracted painfully in his chest. "Yes, he called me. I didn't pick up."

Daniel's cell phone had been in his pocket when the police found his body. The last call had been to Josh. Josh still had the saved message on his voice mail. He didn't have the heart to erase the message, but he also couldn't listen to the sound of Daniel's voice again.

He'd heard the message once, right after being informed of Daniel's murder. Daniel had caught a call on a lead that might be something big and had wanted Josh to get "off his duff" and go with him. Daniel hadn't said where or why.

Josh ran a hand through his hair. "Don't you think I regret that every minute of every day?"

He had been wallowing, nursing his bruised ego, trying to come to terms with the breakup and Lexi's accusations, and he had let the call go to voice mail.

What would Serena say if she knew Lexi had been convinced he had feelings, romantic feelings, for her?

He had no intention of ever telling Serena, because doing so would only be painful for them both.

"I don't know. Do you?" she shot back, her voice filled with anger that matched the flames in her eyes.

"Of course I do." He stared at her, not believing her implication. "Daniel wasn't just my coworker but my best friend. I'd have gladly given my life for his."

He felt her doubts and silent accusations like a thousand serrated knives carving him up inside. It was like facing his childhood all over again. He popped open the door, needing air and space. "What kind of unfeeling monster do you think I am?"

He stalked away. He didn't need to hear her response. He already knew her answer.

Serena sat there watching Josh walk toward his ground-floor apartment. She'd hurt him with her words. Regret squeezed her in a forceful grip.

She couldn't control herself where Josh was concerned. Her anger and grief made her tongue sharp, even though she knew better. Working with him these past few months had been excruciating. Every waking moment she struggled to curb her desire to lash out at him for her brother's death.

Logically she knew whomever had hit her brother over the head was responsible for the murder, and she prayed that God would somehow, someday, bring the perp to justice.

But that didn't stop Serena from heaping blame on Josh. He'd admitted to not picking up when Daniel called him for backup. Serena had no idea what Josh had been doing on his day off. For all she knew, his cell phone had been dead. She didn't care.

Josh hadn't been there for Daniel, his partner, her brother.

Now she couldn't trust Josh to be there for her, not when it really counted. No matter how well she and Josh worked together, she could never count on him to have her back.

So what if a voice inside her head whispered she wasn't being fair? So what if everyone deserved a day off? So what if Josh had had her back more times than she could count these past six months?

She couldn't—didn't—trust him.

But she couldn't ignore the fact that they were about to embark on an undercover mission that would require them to at least be civil with each other in private and madly in love in public. Her stomach clenched.

She wasn't sure how she'd pull off the adoring-wife role.

She didn't even know what that looked like. Not on a personal level.

Oh, sure she'd seen some happy couples. Colton and Lisette, Hunter and Annie to name a few. But she didn't have any experience being in love. She'd never taken the time to pursue romance; she'd been too focused on becoming a marshal and being the best one she could be.

The only person she'd ever daydreamed about was the one man she could never have. Josh. But that was long ago, and those feelings didn't matter anymore.

Remembering the lesson her brother taught her about building bridges in relationships, she knew for the sake of the mission she had to mend this riff with Josh. Starting out their pretend marriage angry wouldn't bode well for the success of the operation. So she'd do her part, despite her personal reservations about Josh.

Resigned to what she had to do, she popped the door open and climbed out. She hadn't been to Josh's apartment since before Daniel's death. Daniel had dragged her to a dinner party at Josh's, hoping to set her up with another guest. The man, Les, worked in the D.A.'s office, if she remembered correctly. He'd been nice enough, but she hadn't been interested.

She'd also met Josh's then-girlfriend: a buxom blonde who'd come across as deeply insecure, clinging to Josh as if she'd been afraid someone would steal him away from her. Serena never wanted to be that kind of woman.

The door to Josh's apartment was ajar. He'd known she'd follow him.

Jerk? Or good partner?

She sighed, accepting whatever God had in mind for her, and gently pushed the door open. She walked into the apartment, surveying his domain. An old leather couch, a huge forty-eight-inch flat-screen television and a stack of books made up the living room. The kitchen showed signs of a hasty breakfast. A loaf of bread sat on the counter. A jar of peanut butter sat out with the lid screwed on crooked.

Josh came out of the bathroom carrying a toiletry bag. He glanced up. Surprise widened his eyes, then he gave her a crooked smile. "You startled me. Didn't really expect you to follow me in."

She swallowed her pride and ego to say, "I'm sorry I was so harsh with you. I don't think you're a monster."

His expression softened, but wariness remained in his eyes. "That's good to know." He nodded and disappeared into his bedroom.

Serena sighed, hating the dejected feeling spreading through her. There was no reason for it. This was work, not personal.

Her gaze landed on a framed photo hanging on the wall, and her breath caught. It was a photo of Josh, Daniel and her from a few summers ago. They'd attended a Cardinals game at Busch Stadium. The first baseman had hit a home run into the stands. Josh had caught the ball and promptly given it to her. In the photo Serena was holding the prize while her brother and Josh flanked her. They looked so happy and carefree.

She missed Daniel. Missed the easy camaraderie among the three of them. And, she realized, she missed Josh, too. He'd been a good friend. And she didn't have many of those.

When Josh came out of the bedroom carrying a suitcase and garment bag, she quickly gathered her composure; no sense in him seeing her getting misty and sentimental.

Taking the garment bag from his hand, she retreated out the door back to the car.

Tense silence filled the car on the drive to Serena's condo. She sought something to say but no words formed. The next few days, weeks—she blew out a sharp breath—months were going to be long if the tension didn't ease between them.

When they arrived, Josh opted to wait by the car while she packed her cosmetic case and her essential garments into a small travel bag. She also grabbed running shoes and yoga clothes. She might be portraying a stay-at-home wife, but that didn't mean she would let her exercise regimen go by the wayside. Staying both physically and mentally prepared for any situation that might arise was an important requirement of the marshals.

When she came out, Josh eyed her two small bags. "That's it?"

"Did you not catch the part about my needing to buy clothing appropriate for this charade?"

"I didn't think you were serious," he replied, taking her bag from her hand and tucking it behind the driver's seat. "We can hit the Galleria on the way."

"Perfect." Three major retailers had stores in the Richmond Heights area mall. Definitely places the affluent wife of a bank executive would shop.

"We'll also need rings," Josh said.

Her stomach dropped. She'd forgotten that part.

Two hours later, with shiny rings, enough clothes to last for the duration of their pretend marriage and two brand-new BMWs, they pulled into the driveway of the detached garage behind the Compton Heights home that would be their base of operation.

Serena climbed out of the small sports utility vehicle they'd decided would be a good mom car. Josh had chosen a roomy four-door sedan. Something unfamiliar fluttered in her tummy. The thought of being a mom stirred places inside her heart she'd not known existed.

Entering the house, Serena was struck by the grandness of the old historic home. Period woodwork throughout, golden oak floors and an ornate staircase leading to the second story took her breath away. The furnishings left behind by the previous occupants matched the historic feel of the place.

"You're here," a woman said as she exited the kitchen. Compact and tiny, with graying hair and a wide smile, she grasped Serena's hand. "I was beginning to worry. I'm Linda."

"Serena."

Linda raised a gray eyebrow. "Susan," she corrected.

Serena flushed. "Yes, Susan."

Patting her hand, Linda said, "You'll get used to it." Then she moved to Josh. "You're as handsome as ever, Jack," she said, using Josh's alias.

Josh smiled and hugged Linda. "You haven't changed a bit, either, Aunt Linda."

"Retirement suits me," Linda said. "However, I have to say, I couldn't resist coming out of retirement to help take down a baby-smuggling ring. The very idea of babies being stolen and sold chaps my hide."

"We're glad to have you." Josh set his luggage on the stairs. "Before we do anything else, let's set up our initial meeting with Matilda Munders."

Anticipation churned in Serena's stomach as they followed Linda into the office. An antique oak desk dominated the room. On top of the desk was a recording system attached to a phone. Josh consulted the file on the Perfect Family Adoption Agency and dialed the number, putting the call on speaker. A moment later the receptionist answered. Josh asked for Matilda.

"One moment, please."

The sound of ringing filled the office. After the third ring, a woman answered.

"Perfect Family Adoption Agency, Matilda speaking. How may I help you?"

Josh met Serena's gaze as he spoke. "I hope you can. My name is Jack Andrews. My wife and I recently relocated to St. Louis. We were told your agency was the one to call. We are desperate to adopt a baby."

"You have called the right place," Matilda said. "Let's schedule an appointment. When can you and your wife come in?"

"This afternoon?"

"Three would be perfect. We'll see you then."

Josh disconnected. "Are you ready, Susan?"

Serena inhaled and let it out slowly. "I'm ready, Jack."

Ready to take down Fred Munders and the Perfect Family Adoption Agency.

Unease slithered down her spine. So many people had died trying to keep the authorities from bringing Munders and the adoption agency to justice.

Serena prayed there would be no more casualties.

FOUR

"Stop fidgeting. You look beautiful, the perfect wife and wannabe mother. And the red suits you," Josh said, pausing at the steps leading to the entrance of the Perfect Family Adoption Agency. He shifted the metal briefcase full of marked hundreds from one hand to the other. "Of course, you always look beautiful."

Serena's hands stilled on the skirt of her floral summer dress. Was Josh mocking her?

She forced her gaze to meet his. The genuine male appreciation in his warm eyes behind the black hipster-framed glasses—which, along with his newly dyed black hair, made her think of Clark Kent—and the soft smile curving his well-formed mouth made heat creep up her neck to settle in her cheeks. She couldn't remember the last time she'd blushed. The sensations rocketing through her weren't unpleasant.

Josh thought she looked beautiful?

She swallowed the sudden lump in her throat. She didn't wear dresses often, only on special occasions and never something as flowy as what she wore now. She preferred tailored, professional attire. Power suits that made her look and feel capable.

But the salesclerk had said the A-line silhouette flattered her figure. Serena guessed "Susan Andrews" would wear a dress that flattered her figure. Serena had to admit she felt feminine in the flowery dress, a coral-colored cap-sleeved shrug and strappy wedge heels.

But the biggest change had been the haircut. Linda had convinced her she needed to go shorter and dye her dark brown hair a light shade of auburn. She'd hardly recognized herself in the mirror. The bob curling around her chin emphasized her eyes and the length of her jaw. And the wispy bangs brushing across her forehead would take getting used to.

She dropped her gaze from Josh's and stared at her bright pink painted nails. Another first.

Not sure what to do with his statement or how to feel about her reaction to his words, she straightened her shoulders and fought for the professional persona that had served her well over the course of her career. She was a marshal doing a job. And the man beside her was her partner. This was all pretend.

She must never forget that.

"Thank you, Jo—Jack."

Josh grinned. "You're welcome, *Susan*." He held out his arm. "Shall we see about adopting a baby?"

She hesitated, chewing on her lower lip. Could she convince Mrs. Munders they were a loving couple? Could she act like she adored Josh? So much was riding on their effectively gaining Mrs. Munders's trust so they could catch her and her husband in the act of illegally selling a baby to them. Her heart cramped.

"You'll do fine," Josh whispered, taking her hand and tucking her arm through his.

His uncanny ability to read her left her mouth dry. She averted her gaze from his probing brown eyes. She prayed he was right. She would need God's strength to convince anyone they were a devoted couple.

She stared at the brick single-story building before her,

trying not to quake. Pretending to be a married woman in love wanting a child was completely out of her wheelhouse. She'd rather be chasing down a bad guy on the street. Where was her well-earned professionalism when she needed it?

The place looked well maintained. Flower beds filled with blooming roses and azaleas lined the concrete stairs leading to the entrance. A knot in her shoulders tightened with each step she took toward the entrance.

Josh ushered her through the glass door, his hand skimming over her lower back. She quickened her step to outpace his touch and the ensuing tingles racing over her.

The reception area was small with six chairs, a coffee table covered with magazines and a desk behind which sat a young, blonde-haired woman in her mid-twenties. A name plaque read Jill Treehill.

Jill smiled, showing pearl-white teeth behind ruby-red lips. "Welcome. How can I help you?"

"We have an appointment with Mrs. Munders," Josh said.

"Just one moment." Jill gracefully rose from the desk and glided down the hall to the closed door on the right.

She returned a few moments later. "Mrs. Munders will see you now."

They were escorted down a short hall to an office. Serena stopped short when her gaze landed on a collage of baby photos covering the wall opposite the door. Her heart lurched. How many of these little faces were children ripped away from their parents and sold to other families?

Josh touched her elbow. She started, swinging her gaze to the woman rising from behind the desk. Petite, with gray hair in a bun and a kindly face wreathed in wrinkles. Pale blue eyes regarded Josh for a moment before turning to Serena.

Mrs. Munders's eyes widened. "Jeannie, darling, where have you been?"

Taken aback, Serena shared a confused glance with Josh.

"Mrs. Munders," Josh said. "I'm Jack Andrews and this is my wife, Susan. We have an appointment with you."

Confusion clouded Mrs. Munders's eyes. She blinked several times and then said, "Please have a seat." She gestured to two chairs facing the desk, her gaze never leaving Serena.

They sat. Josh tucked the briefcase under the chair. Serena folded her hands together to keep from fidgeting. Josh placed his big, warm hand over hers. She shivered from the electric current zinging up her arm. Her first impulse was to pull away but she forced herself to remain still.

Mrs. Munders smiled. "What can I do for you?"

"We want to adopt a baby," Josh stated. "We've been married for five years now and have been unable to conceive."

The sympathy in Mrs. Munders's eyes had Serena threading her fingers through Josh's to keep from reaching across the desk and shaking the money-grubbing woman. The sympathy couldn't be real. Not with all they'd learned about the Munderses and their illegal organization.

Instead, Serena sat forward and played to the feigned emotion in the older woman's gaze. "I really would like to be a mother."

The words sounded sincere even to her own ears. A desire for children, for a family, bubbled inside Serena. She pushed the distracting sentiment back into a dark corner of her mind and concentrated on the woman sitting across the desk. Now was not the time to think about herself and her lack of a love life.

Mrs. Munders nodded. "Of course you do, dear. Well,

you've come to the right place. We have had hundreds of successful adoptions over the years."

Hundreds of adoptions? Serena's gaze drifted to the photo board as a sick feeling churned in her midsection. A gentle tug on her hand by Josh gave her the strength to refocus.

"I have forms you'll need to fill out," Mrs. Munders continued. "And then we'll schedule individual interviews and a home visit."

Serena swallowed. "Individual interviews?"

"Yes. I like to talk to each parent to get a feel for who they are apart from their partner." She turned her gaze to Josh. "I like to see how the house is set up for a child, the yard and neighborhood. We can't be too careful. I take placing children in adoptive homes very seriously."

"That's good to know," Josh said in a neutral tone.

But Serena could see the angry tic of muscle in the side of his jaw. No doubt he was thinking of the babies taken from their mothers through coercion. The thought made Serena's blood boil as well, but she kept a tight rein on her emotions.

Mrs. Munders opened a desk drawer and withdrew a manila envelope. "The first step will be filling out the application. There is an application fee of five thousand dollars. Cash up front."

"Of course," Josh said and reached for the briefcase. He popped the lid and counted out the money. Mrs. Munders stuffed the stack of bills in a drawer, then made a notation in a ledger before offering Josh an envelope with the application inside.

"How long will the process take?" Serena asked.

Mrs. Munders smiled kindly. "It could take up to a year."

Serena winced and cast a frantic glance at Josh. No way could she keep up the facade of Susan Andrews for a year.

"We'd like to expedite the process," Josh said. "We are anxious to start our family."

"I understand," Mrs. Munders replied. "We will do our best to find you the perfect child as soon as possible."

"I'd like an infant," Serena said, thinking about Baby Kay. Where was the little girl now? Was she safe? Being cared for? Concern squeezed Serena's heart.

"That will cost more," Mrs. Munders said, her shrewd gaze on Serena.

Of course it would. Every time they ordered off the menu, the price went up. Red flags blazed in Serena's mind.

"What is the price?" Serena asked, careful to keep her face from showing how much she detested the idea of buying a baby.

"Doesn't matter how much money," Josh stated before Mrs. Munders could respond. "My wife wants a baby and I'll pay whatever it costs."

"Excellent." Mrs. Munders opened a ledger on her desk and wrote down their names by hand.

Her old-school way of keeping track of clients would make tracking down the babies and their adoptive parents harder. And if they asked for a warrant, the leak in the department would be able to warn the Munderses.

Subtly straining to see the names listed, Serena couldn't make out a single word. Mrs. Munders's shaky handwriting was illegible at this angle. Serena fiddled with the hem of her sweater.

They had to get a look at that ledger.

Josh placed his hand over hers again. She jerked slightly at the contact. Hopefully, Mrs. Munders didn't notice.

"I can see how anxious you are, Susan," Mrs. Munders said.

Rats! Serena tried for a smile but was sure it turned out to be more of a grimace. "This has been a trying time."

In so many ways. Her brother had been murdered. Innocent babies were being bought and sold like chattel. And she was pretending to be Josh's wife so they could "start" a family. Her stomach curdled.

Her face wreathed in what had to be artificial concern, Mrs. Munders rose and came around the desk.

If Serena didn't know the truth about this woman, she might believe Mrs. Munders actually cared, that her heart was truly pierced by the pain of those who sat across from her each day desperate for a child.

Mrs. Munders held out her hand.

Compelled to take the offered compassion or appear rude, Serena placed her hand into the older woman's. Mrs. Munders's skin was soft and smooth, her bones fragile in Serena's grip. Yet there didn't seem to be anything soft about this woman.

"Don't worry, my dear Jeannie," Mrs. Munders crooned. "I will take care of everything. You'll have a child in your arms before you know it."

That was the second time she'd referred to Serena by the name of Jeannie.

"I'm Susan. Who's Jeannie?"

Panic marched across Mrs. Munders's face. She recoiled slightly, her gaze focusing on Serena. "Oh, dear. I'm so sorry. It's just you look so much like my daughter."

Surprised sympathy tugged at Serena. She remembered from the background check that the Munderses had had a daughter who passed away years ago. "What happened to Jeannie?"

"A car accident. She was twenty. She had auburn hair like yours."

Serena couldn't help sending Josh a quick glance, but his gaze was fixed on Mrs. Munders, his expression appropriately sympathetic but intent.

Mrs. Munders gave herself a little shake. "Forgive me."

She paused, cocked her head and said, "What was it you wanted?"

"We gave you the money," Josh supplied.

Serena tucked in her chin. "You gave us the adoption application."

"Oh, right." She let go of Serena's hand. "You two fill out the application. Then we can schedule a home visit."

"Does your husband handle the legal paperwork?" Josh asked. "Will we receive a receipt for the amount we've paid?"

Serena watched Mrs. Munders's reaction closely. The woman didn't miss a beat. "Yes, he does. And I'm sure you will be given a receipt."

Josh sat forward. "When will we be able to meet with him?"

"Oh, not until I've vetted your application and we have a child available," came Mrs. Munders's reply.

The expression of utter confidence grated on Serena's nerves. Obviously the woman believed she and her husband were beyond the law's reach. *We'll see about that,* Serena thought.

Josh rose. "We'll be in touch."

Serena stood and hesitated. She wanted a look at the ledger. "Could I use your restroom?"

"Of course, dear," Mrs. Munders said and walked to the door. "At the end of the hall on the right."

Serena met Josh's confused gaze. Keeping her back to Mrs. Munders, she raised a hand in front of her and pointed one finger toward the ledger on the desk. Since the woman left the book open and in plain sight, Serena had no qualms about taking a peek.

A frown appeared on Josh's face then quickly disappeared as he apparently realized her intent. One corner of his mouth lifted and he gave her a subtle nod. He placed his hand at the small of her back, sending those little tingles shimmering up her spine again. He ushered her into the hall.

"I'll only be a moment," Serena said and walked down the hall toward the restrooms.

"Mrs. Munders, would you be so kind as to take a look at our new vehicle?" Josh asked. "We bought it with a baby in mind."

"Of course I can," Mrs. Munders replied in a pleased tone.

Serena slowed and waited until they'd disappeared into the reception area. She heard them talking to Jill before going out the front door. Quickly Serena darted back into Mrs. Munders's office and hurried to the desk. The ledger sat open on the desktop. She fished out her smartphone from her purse and snapped a picture of the page. She flipped back a page and took a snapshot of that one, too. Then, fearing she was running out of time, she hurried from the office and entered the reception room as Josh and Mrs. Munders were coming back inside.

"That is a lovely vehicle, and I can already tell you two will make great parents," Mrs. Munders exclaimed with a wide smile.

Josh took Serena's hand. She started to pull away but noticed Mrs. Munders's interested gaze. She tightened her hold and leaned into him.

"We'll be in touch soon," Serena called out.

They left Mrs. Munders standing in the doorway of the Perfect Family Adoption Agency.

Once in the car, Serena sat back with a sigh. "That was stressful."

"You're going to have to stop acting like a skittish colt every time I touch you."

Her defenses rose. "I don't."

But she had. And she didn't know how to stop. For the past year and a half she'd harbored so much animosity toward Josh that letting it go was hard. Especially when his touches sparked such delicious shivers and tingles.

Josh snorted.

Hoping to steer the conversation back to the situation, she said, "I snapped photos of a couple pages in the ledger. Though the woman's handwriting is nearly impossible to read. I also got some shots of the baby collage on the wall."

"She was a bit of an odd duck," Josh commented.

"I'm not sure what to think of her," Serena said. "She seemed a little confused. Yet I saw glimpses of a sharp intellect."

"An act? Or old age?"

"That's the million-dollar question, isn't it?"

"We'll find out." Josh's gaze traveled over her face and softened before meeting her eye. He turned back to the road. "She picked up on how uncomfortable you were."

Serena blew out a frustrated breath. "I'm sure she attributes my nervousness to wanting to adopt."

"Maybe." He changed lanes in the heavy St. Louis traffic. "One way or another she and her husband are going down, and I don't care if she is certifiable."

"You don't mean that, do you?"

Josh pulled up to a red light. "The illegal adoptions have been going on for a long time. We've barely scratched the surface. And there's no way I'd believe the woman doesn't know what's happening within her own company."

He had a point. The agency belonged to her, while her husband brokered the deals on the back end by securing babies for adoption. She had to know what her husband was up to. Didn't she?

Didn't husbands and wives share everything?

She mentally scoffed. She had no idea what a successful marriage entailed. All she'd ever seen of her parents' marriage was the bickering and fighting, which had escalated to all-out war by the time she was ten. Then a messy divorce that left her feeling adrift.

If she hadn't had Daniel as her anchor… Her heart compressed with grief. Her fists curled as her sorrow morphed into simmering anger. Daniel shouldn't be dead. If only Josh had answered his phone!

When Josh pulled up to the cover house, she jumped out and hurried inside as fast as her wedge sandals would allow. A stab of guilt for leaving Josh in the dust impaled her. She mentally took a step back. She needed to get a grip on her emotions around him.

"Hmm, something smells good," he said as he stepped into the entryway behind her, filling the room with a low-level buzz that set Serena's blood to humming.

The house smelled of savory spices and grilling meat. Suddenly, her mouth watered. She could get used to having someone preparing meals for her. Her culinary skills barely included scrambled eggs and toast. Learning to cook had always been a low priority on her list of things to accomplish. Good thing they had Linda around to cook or they might starve.

"How did it go?" Linda came out of the kitchen, wiping her hands on a bright blue apron with yellow ducks all over it.

"It could have been better." Serena dug out the smartphone. "I took some pictures of a ledger that was on Mrs. Munders's desk. Do you think you could try to decipher it?"

"Of course." Linda made no move to take the phone. "My hands are greasy. Set the phone on the desk in the office."

She pivoted, nearly toppling over Josh, and headed for the office with her phone, eager to get away from him. She heard Linda say, "So I hear it could have gone better."

"You could say that."

Serena made a face and dropped the phone onto the desk. She didn't like the idea of their discussing her behind her back, but she had no intention of joining them so they could analyze her behavior. Especially when she herself didn't understand why she reacted the way she did around Josh and was struggling to control her reactions.

She headed upstairs to her room at the end of the hall. Kicking off the sandals, she sank down on the window seat and stared out over the lush backyard. She could picture a play structure in the corner and a sandpit near the edge of the patio. What would it be like to have a house full of children? And a husband to love?

Josh's image rose in her mind. His brown eyes so warm and inviting. His strong jawline and his straight nose so appealing. With a little thrill she remembered the way he'd looked at her when he'd told her she was beautiful. As if he'd meant it. And she'd wanted to believe him.

Her pretend husband.

The man she blamed for her brother's death.

She tried to banish Josh from her thoughts but he wouldn't go.

No matter how much she wished otherwise, she was stuck with Josh as a partner, and she was going to have to figure out a way to deal with it.

She bowed her head and whispered, "Lord, give me strength."

"You need to go talk to her."

Josh inhaled sharply. Easy for Linda to say. She could never understand how each time he looked at Serena, his guilt over Daniel's death dug a deeper trench through him. He opened his mouth to protest.

Linda held up a hand. "You two have to work this out. If she's jumpy around you, people will notice and start to ask questions. You two have been partners for over six months now. I don't understand what the problem is."

"She blames me for Daniel's death and sometimes it gets the better of her," Josh said, putting it baldly. "The truth is, I *am* to blame. I should have been with him that day."

Linda laid a hand on his arm. "I read the case file. You could no more predict what happened than you could have prevented it."

Josh appreciated her attempt at assuaging his guilt but if he'd answered the phone that day, if he hadn't taken a personal day, if Lexi hadn't picked then to break up with him, if he'd been able to give his heart to Lexi, then Daniel would still be alive.

He shook his head at the futility of his thoughts. *Ifs* would only drive him crazy. He had to stay focused on the moment and on the job. And that meant figuring out a way for him and Serena to work together to build a believable cover as a happy couple. But how?

Obviously, he'd failed with Lexi.

The only example he had of a happy, loving couple were his grandparents on his mother's side. Both were long gone now, and his memories had faded to general impressions. Grandpa helping Gran in the kitchen. Bringing her gifts. Holding her hand as they walked through the neighborhood.

His own parents' marriage had dissolved when he was too young to have paid much attention. *Dissolved,* that was such a polite way of putting it. More like his father had destroyed their lives, and a whole lot of other people's lives, when he embezzled from the company he worked for and died in prison two years later.

Josh ran a hand through his hair. "I don't know how to make her comfortable with me."

"I'll go talk to her." Linda untied the apron and headed

for the stairs. "My suggestion, Josh, is to court her," she said over her shoulder and then walked away.

Josh blinked at the older agent's retreating back. Court Serena?

For a pretend relationship in a pretend marriage.

Trouble was, how did he do that without either of them getting hurt?

The light tap at the door jolted Serena to her feet. Josh?

Tension tightened the muscles between her shoulder blades. She supposed they would have to talk and figure out how to keep this charade going at some point. But did it have to be now? Couldn't he wait until tomorrow or the next day? She knew she wasn't being realistic.

The sooner they worked out the kinks in this farce of a marriage, the sooner they could bring this assignment to fruition. Which was the ultimate goal. A goal she believed in.

She padded barefoot to the door and cracked it open.

Linda smiled at her. "May I come in?"

Relieved, Serena opened the door so Linda could enter.

"So what's the problem?" Linda asked without preamble.

Moving back to the window seat, Serena said, "Which problem?"

Linda followed her to the window. "There's more than one?"

"We have a leak in the department." Serena held up one finger. "Babies are being taken from their mothers and sold illegally." She held up a second finger. "I have to pretend to be Josh's loving wife." She held up a third finger. "And I can't seem to figure out how to solve any of these problems." She dropped her hand to her side.

"The leak in the department is a quandary that will eventually be resolved," Linda said, holding up one finger. "That's Chief Harrison's responsibility, not yours. You and Josh are doing something about the illegal adoption ring." She held up a second finger and then a third. "But the success of the assignment before you depends on your ability to play the loving wife."

Serena groaned and jumped to her feet. "I know. And that's *the* problem."

"Because you blame him for your brother's death."

Meeting Linda's steady gaze, she nodded. "Yes."

Linda sat on the window seat and patted the bench next to her. Sighing, Serena sat and prepared herself for a lecture on how to do her job.

"Look, I can't pretend to understand why you blame Josh, but I do know Josh is a good guy."

Serena frowned. "He didn't answer my brother's call for help. If he had, Daniel wouldn't be dead."

Linda shook her head. "Honey, you don't know that. They *both* could have ended up dead."

Acid roiled in Serena's gut. She didn't like the thought of them both gone. "But why? That's what torments me. Why was Daniel in that alley? What led him there without backup?"

"We'll never know until the perps are caught," Linda stated. "Right now our concern has to be *this* assignment. You have to put your anger and grief away for now."

"I've been trying to ever since I was partnered with Josh. But I'm struggling to trust him. Trust he'll be there for me if I need him."

"Ah, I see." Linda narrowed her gaze and stared at Serena with an intensity that made Serena want to squirm. "Has he given you any concrete reason to distrust him?"

Frustrated with the question and the only answer she could give, she blew out a breath. "No."

Linda inclined her head. "That's a start. What was your relationship with Josh like before Daniel's death?"

Serena thought back to those days. "We were friends." She dropped her gaze to her clenched hands. "I sort of had a crush on him."

Linda chuckled. "Really?"

Serena's gaze shot to the older woman.

Linda's eyebrows rose. "Well, that's something we can work with." She laid a hand on Serena's forearm. "Let's tap into those feelings."

Serena started to shake her head. Those feelings were long dead. She froze. Or were they? Memories of all the little ways she'd reacted to Josh screamed through her brain. Ways that had nothing to do with her anger or resentment over Josh's part in her brother's death, but everything to do with an attraction to her *pretend* husband she couldn't deny.

Fine. She could tap into the attraction for the sake of the mission and nothing else. But she wouldn't let her heart become involved. That would be a huge mistake she was determined not to make, no matter how much she melted every time Josh was near.

FIVE

The chime of the doorbell echoed through the house. The sound jarred through Serena, rousing unease. Who would be visiting them? No one knew they were here.

"That's my cue," Linda said and hustled from the room to answer the front door.

Serena glanced out the bedroom window overlooking the front of the house. There was no car in the driveway and no new vehicles parked at the curb on the street. Curious and cautious, she retrieved her service weapon from her purse and hurried out of the bedroom. She paused on the landing, her gun tucked behind her leg in the folds of her skirt.

Josh stood at the bottom of the staircase with his back to her, his weapon held at his side, his finger against the slide. Linda's hand curled over the doorknob. She glanced at Josh and then at Serena, gave a sharp nod, then opened the door wide enough to talk to the person outside, but not wide enough to reveal Josh's or Serena's positions.

"Can I help you?" Linda said.

"Hi, I'm Trina Johnson from next door," a female voice said from the other side of the door. She had a bit of a Texas twang in her tone. "I thought I'd stop in and introduce myself and say welcome to the neighborhood."

"How kind," Linda said. "I'm Linda Andrews. Won't you come in?"

Serena rolled her shoulders, letting relief sweep in. She walked back to her room to put her piece in the top dresser drawer. When she went downstairs she found Josh and a blonde-haired woman in the living room. Serena guessed the woman to be in her mid-thirties. Her green eyes regarded Serena with curiosity and friendliness.

Josh held out his hand to Serena as she entered the room. "Ah, here's my wife."

Taking his hand, she noted how his palm fit snugly against hers and sent a little shiver up her arm. She swallowed and produced a smile that she hoped didn't look fake.

"Susan, this is Trina Johnson from next door," Josh said.

Serena held out her free hand. "Hello, Trina. It's nice to meet you."

"Likewise," Trina said, giving Serena's hand a shake. "Your husband was telling me you're from Alaska. I've never been that far north."

Neither had Serena. "Yes, it's lovely. Are you from St. Louis?"

Trina shook her head. "Dallas. My Darrell and I moved here four years ago. You'll like the neighborhood. Everyone's real friendly."

"Are there many kids in the neighborhood?" Josh asked.

"Young children?" Serena added.

"Oh, my, yes. I think almost everyone has kids, from infant to late teens in age. Ours are six and eight. Both boys. Do y'all have little ones?"

Josh squeezed Serena's hand. Serena smiled at Trina. "Not yet. But we're in the process of adopting."

"How wonderful," Trina said. "I believe one or two of the Frellners' kids are adopted."

Serena's heart rate picked up. She tightened her hold on Josh's hand. They exchanged a glance. "How old are their children?"

Trina scrunched up her nose. "I don't know which ones are adopted and which are their biological kids. They're a blended family, so some are hers and some his and then they have one or two together."

"How many kids do they have?" Josh asked.

"Six or seven." Trina waved a hand. "You'll meet them all on Saturday at the neighborhood get-together."

"Get-together?" Serena said at the same time as Josh said, "Saturday?"

Serena met Josh's gaze. His mouth tipped up at the corner.

"At the start of every summer we have a neighborhood barbecue," Trina explained. "We ask everyone to park in their driveways or garages, and close off the streets. We gather in the intersection. Bill and Judy and Garry and Charlene drag out their barbecues. The homeowners association provides the hamburgers and plates, utensils, et cetera. Then each family brings a side dish to share. It's a great time, and it gives us all a chance to build community into our busy lives."

"That sounds like fun," Josh said. "We wouldn't miss it for the world."

Serena nodded though her stomach dropped. Panic fluttered in her chest. It was one thing to pretend to be a married couple for an audience of one—but for the whole neighborhood? Her throat constricted. How could she possibly convince so many people at once?

"Great," Trina said. She glanced around. "We'll miss George and Marsha." Her gaze came back to Serena. "The Zanettis were nice people. His transfer was so sudden, they didn't even take their furniture, which I see you've kept…." She trailed off, her unease and curiosity palpable.

Josh jumped in. "They rented the house to us furnished, which worked out well for us. Moving a household from Alaska would have been very expensive."

A smile of amusement twitched at Serena's lips. Josh was so smooth and quick-witted. Traits that had drawn her to him when they first met. Traits she still found appealing. She averted her gaze.

"I could imagine so," Trina replied. "The Zanettis always hosted the neighborhood Christmas party." She pointed toward the picture window. "They'd put a tree there. Marsha made the best homemade eggnog."

The expectant look in Trina's eyes prompted Serena to say, "I'll talk to Aunt Linda. She's the cook in the family." She shared a look with Josh. "I'm sure we could do a Christmas party."

Josh lifted her hand to his lips. "Whatever you want, darling."

An involuntary tremor raced up her arm and settled behind her breastbone. She blinked at Josh. He held her gaze with a soft smile. Her heart tripped over itself. A heated flush spread through her. Didn't this house have air-conditioning?

Trina smiled. "Well, I'll take my leave now, but I hope you know if you need anything, I'm in the house on the left."

They walked Trina to the front door. Josh's arm snaked around Serena's waist and pulled her in close. She inhaled sharply as each muscle in her body tensed, and an unexpected thrill skated over her flesh. Forcing herself to relax, she leaned into his side like a loving wife would. The feel of him, the masculine scent of him, filled her head and made her knees weak.

"Thank you for coming over," Serena said. "It was good to meet you."

"Likewise," Trina responded. She headed down the porch steps with a wave. "See you Saturday."

"What time is the barbecue?" Josh called.

Trina stopped on the sidewalk. "We start gathering around four in the afternoon."

"Perfect. We'll see you then." Josh tugged Serena back inside and closed the door.

Serena let out a pent-up breath. "That went well."

She tried to step away but he held her firmly against his side.

"Thank you," he said.

"For?"

"Doing such a good job pretending to like me." He released her. "I hope it wasn't too difficult for you."

There was the faintest hint of sarcasm in his tone. Her eyebrows rose. He'd expected her to blow it, like she'd almost done in Mrs. Munders's office. She was happy to disappoint him. "Not too difficult."

One side of his mouth lifted. "Good. Then Saturday shouldn't be a problem."

Of course it would be a problem, but she held the words in. She couldn't let on how freaked out she was by the prospect of performing for a whole group of people who would be expecting to see a couple in love.

After a heartbeat, Josh said, "We have work to do. I'll check in with the chief and let him know we've made contact with Mrs. Munders and have Linda find out more about the Frellners."

Pulling her focus back to the case, she nodded. "I'll contact the Houston marshals to see if they've managed to extract any more information out of the suspect I shot."

Josh gave an approving nod. "Sounds like a plan."

She watched him walk away and wondered why his approval made her feel so good. His opinion didn't matter. Not in the least. With grim determination, she squashed the swell of pleasure and made her calls.

* * *

"Good job," Chief Harrison said. "Keep me apprised of the situation and be careful."

"We will. Thanks, Chief." Josh hung up the phone as Serena entered the den carrying a duffel bag. His heart squeezed tight within the wall of his chest. She'd changed back into her tailored suit, and there was a grim set to her mouth. Even her new hairdo had been tamed.

He missed the softer look she had adopted for their interview with Mrs. Munders. Though as he'd told her earlier, either way she was a beautiful woman. He'd have to be without a pulse to not be attracted to her. But he could, however, control that attraction, no matter how much he'd enjoyed pretending to be her husband when their neighbor had shown up unannounced.

He brought himself up short. The only reason he'd enjoyed the charade was because, for once, they had been free of the tension that was always strung tight between them.

"What are you doing?" he asked.

"We've got a lead," she said without preamble.

"On?"

"The two guys who escaped." She walked over to the window and glanced out to the front street, checking the neighborhood.

"The guy you shot gave them up?" That was a surprise. The guy had stonewalled them, and Josh had figured he'd keep up the silent act indefinitely.

She turned and shook her head. "No. But the Houston marshals checked the cameras in the area and caught a suspicious-looking van entering the McIntyre neighborhood a little before the three amigos broke into the house, and then the camera showed the van burning rubber out of the neighborhood a little while later."

"Okay." That was progress. "I assume they put a BOLO

out on the van?" A Be On the Look Out notice would go out to all law enforcement agencies across the country. It would only be a matter of time before the van attracted attention.

"They did." She gave him a smug smile. "And the van showed up here in St. Louis."

"What?"

"Yep. A patrol over in the Sixth District spotted the van tucked in an alley. They have officers sitting on it."

"Rough area." Josh's blood thrummed. "That's why you're in your own clothes."

"Bingo. Let's go."

"We can't," he said. "You know that, right? It would blow our cover."

"If we take these guys into custody and flip them, then this whole charade could end today."

And that was what she wanted. He wasn't sure why that stung. He wanted this to be over quickly, too.

"Just so you don't think I haven't thought about our cover," she said, digging into the duffel bag and handing him a baseball cap with the U.S. Marshals emblem and a pair of dark sunglasses. Then she pulled out another set of the same. With the hat on her head, her hair tucked up under the rim and the dark glasses, she could be any number of female marshals.

Josh conceded her the point and donned the hat and glasses.

Serena tossed him a set of keys. "Linda said we could take her car. Less conspicuous."

"Good thinking." He led the way to the garage, where Linda's older-model Buick sedan was parked next to Jack Andrews's BMW.

Josh spared a glance at the luxury car before sliding in behind the wheel of the sedan. "You don't suppose the chief would let me keep that car, do you?"

Serena barked out a short laugh. "Hardly."

The drive to the Sixth District, north of downtown St. Louis, took longer than Josh had expected. The late-afternoon traffic was heavy as people fled their jobs, intent on returning to their suburban homes.

He found the address the patrol officer had given to Serena. He drove past the nondescript white van, which had been parked and half hidden behind a Dumpster. Its right back bumper stuck out, which was what attracted the officer's attention.

Josh parked the sedan a few blocks down, and he and Serena climbed out. Keeping close to the building they made their way to the van. Josh saw the undercover car with two law enforcement officers positioned opposite the alley, where they had a clear view of anyone coming or going from the van. Josh and Serena crossed the street and went to the passenger side of the unmarked car.

The plain-clothed officer in the passenger seat rolled down his window. A badge hung around his neck on a leather string. "You the U.S. marshals?"

"We are." Josh flashed his badge. "McCall and Summers."

"Bergman and Trudy," the officer said. "With the Sixth District patrol."

Serena flashed her badge. "Has there been any movement?"

"None," the older officer replied. "Could be abandoned or they could be holed up inside one of the buildings on either side."

"What are those buildings?" Josh asked, studying the boxy brick structures that made up most of the business parks throughout the city.

"The one on the right is a warehouse for a manufacturing plant. The one on the left has a printing company downstairs and several financial offices upstairs."

"Not likely the building on the left," Josh said, as Serena said, "The warehouse is more likely."

After a beat, Serena said, "Let's check it out."

"You want backup?" Bergman asked.

"Would appreciate it." Serena turned and walked across the street.

Frustration crimped Josh's stomach. She still didn't fully trust him. After the past six months of working together, why hadn't she figured out he wouldn't let anything happen to her? He owed it to Daniel to keep his sister safe.

Josh watched as she strode away in this graffiti-tagged part of town in her uptown suit and squared-away hair. Something shifted and contracted within his chest. He owed it to *himself* to keep her safe.

"You two take the back entrance," Josh directed the officers. "We'll take the front."

He jogged to catch up to Serena. "Hey, let's be smart about this. We can't bust down the door without probable cause."

"The van was seen fleeing a crime scene. That's your probable cause," she said. Placing her hand on her weapon she approached the front entrance.

Shaking his head, Josh followed. She was rash and bold and amazing. If he weren't careful he'd find himself falling for her. Something he couldn't let happen. For her sake as well as his.

A square plate of glass provided a view inside. Josh gazed over Serena's head. Inside, large shadowed shapes were barely visible in the unlit warehouse. Serena tried the knob. The door popped open.

She gave him a triumphant glance. He acknowledged it with a nod.

Withdrawing his weapon from the holster beneath his jacket, he stepped past Serena to lead the way inside the warehouse.

It took a moment for his eyes to adjust to the gloomy shadows and inky blackness of the cavernous building. He removed the small handheld flashlight from the clip on his belt. Serena did the same. The beams of their lights illuminated large crates stacked two or three high.

Leading with his weapon, he made his way farther into the yawning space. Serena kept pace to his right. The crates gave way to machine parts gathered in haphazard piles. He forged ahead, stepping over a carburetor.

A whisper of movement behind him raised the fine hairs at the back of his neck.

He spun around, shining his flashlight into the darkness. No one there.

His partner was gone.

Fear arced through him, making his heart pound and his blood race. Was she okay? Had he failed her? "Serena!"

His voice echoed off the brick walls. Anxiety clawed through him, tightening the muscles in his shoulders, his neck, his throat. Breathing became difficult. He could not lose another partner. Guilt over Daniel's death stabbed him like a physical blow. He had to find Serena.

He hurried past the mounds of metal and gears to the far end of the warehouse. The beam of the flashlight zipped back and forth as he searched for Serena. The shadows closed in on him. Would he find Serena's broken body?

A light bobbed behind a drop cloth suspended from hooks jutting from the overhead beam.

He yanked the curtain aside.

The beam of his flashlight landed on Serena. He breathed out his relief and anger rushed in to take its place.

"We found one of them." Her flashlight trained on a mattress lying on the floor revealing a body. Lifeless eyes stared up at them. A gaping wound in the middle of the man's chest was crusted with dried blood.

Ignoring the dead body, Josh gripped her elbow. "What

were you thinking? You left your position." She'd gone off on her own, just like her brother. And that had turned out to be a deadly decision. A shudder worked through him.

"I saw something, so I peeled off." She shook off his hand. "Obviously they've been using this place as a hide-out." She swung the beam of her light over empty take-out cartons.

Reining in his anger, he kicked aside a soda can and reached down to check the pockets of the man lying on the mattress. Empty. "I'm calling this in."

Serena put a hand on his arm. "Shhhh. Did you hear that?"

The scuff of a shoe. On the other side of the curtain. They were vulnerable.

Josh grabbed Serena and yanked her down just as the deafening retort of gunfire split the air, accompanied by a blinding muzzle flash. A bullet whizzed over their heads and slammed into the concrete wall behind them.

A door banged open. For a moment light spilled into the warehouse before winking out when the door closed.

Josh jumped up, taking Serena with him. They ran from the curtained makeshift room, nearly ramming into Officers Bergman and Trudy.

"We heard a gunshot. Are you two okay?" Bergman asked.

Their four flashlight beams danced in the darkness.

"Yes," Serena stated. "Did you see which way the suspect went?"

The door at the front of the building opened showing the silhouette of the suspect escaping.

"He's getting away," Josh shouted and raced toward the front entrance.

He hit the door, sending it swinging open. Sunlight assaulted Josh's eyes. He blinked to clear his vision. The squeal of tires on pavement screeched through his head.

He ran for the corner of the building. The white van sped down the alley. Josh fired off a shot and hit the back door. The van swerved drunkenly, then turned at the end of the alley and disappeared from view.

Josh lowered his weapon.

"We have the license plate number," Serena said, halting beside him. "He won't get far."

Josh holstered his weapon with more force than necessary. Frustration pounded at his temples. "So much for ending this assignment today."

They left the police officers to handle the details of the deceased man and returned to the cover house. Josh pulled Linda's car into the garage. As soon as the garage door closed, Serena was out and heading inside before he had his door open. He understood her irritation. She'd expected a better outcome.

"So?" Linda asked when Josh entered the den.

"One got away." He gave Linda the lowdown on the events. A few minutes later, Serena came in wearing running attire. Josh cocked an eyebrow.

Serena shrugged. "Susan Andrews takes care of herself." She stretched her long, lean legs. "I'm going to check out the neighborhood."

"If you'll wait, I'll join you," Josh said. He could use some exercise to burn off the earlier rush of adrenaline.

Ten minutes later, they set out at a steady pace. Serena had her cell phone attached to her arm by a band. They'd agreed that they would only use the burner cell phone for contact with Perfect Family.

"I never run without it," she said, meeting his gaze. "I twisted my ankle once while out on a run and was glad to have it with me to call for help."

Josh didn't have to ask if it had been Daniel she'd called. The way her mouth pursed and her eyes glistened with sadness said it all.

He diverted his gaze to the houses. The high-end neighborhood with manicured lawns, expensive vehicles and children playing in the yards was such the American dream. So different from his own experience.

Serena's phone chimed. She winced. "Oops, forgot to turn off the ringer."

The caller ID identified Bud as the caller.

Slowing their pace, Serena slipped the phone from the band and answered. She listened for a moment then thanked him before clicking off. "That was actually Burke on the line. Bud was driving. They heard about the warehouse incident and wanted to let us know they would be following up with the police department."

Josh hoped Bud and Burke had more success than he and Serena had had.

By the time they returned to the cover house, Josh's back was soaked with sweat. Serena, however, didn't appear at all bothered by the heat or the fast-paced run.

Linda greeted them with tall glasses of lemonade.

The burner cell phone in Josh's pocket rang. A glance at the caller ID sent his heart lurching. The call was coming from the Perfect Family Adoption Agency.

"This is Jack," Josh said.

"Mr. Andrews, this is Matilda Munders of the Perfect Family Adoption Agency."

"Mrs. Munders, this is a surprise," Josh said, his glance meeting Serena's stunned gaze.

"For me, as well," Mrs. Munders stated. "I've recently been informed of an infant in need of a home. I was so taken with your wife that I immediately thought of you two. If there is any way you could fill out the application and bring it by first thing tomorrow morning I may be able to put a child in your arms by the end of the week."

Josh couldn't believe his ears. Apparently his willingness to fork over a large sum of money so easily went a long way to securing a child quicker than expected. "We'll get right on that. I'm sure Susan will be ecstatic."

"Wonderful," Mrs. Munders said. "I look forward to seeing you again."

"We look forward to seeing you, too, and hearing more about this baby," Josh said and hung up.

Excitement revved through his veins. Things on this front were moving more quickly than they'd anticipated. By the end of the week, Josh hoped they would have enough evidence to put Mr. and Mrs. Munders out of the baby-stealing-and-selling business once and for all.

And put an end to his and Serena's fake marriage.

SIX

"Act as if you like each other," Linda directed from behind the lens of the black camera set on a tripod in the middle of the living room.

Serena chewed the inside of her lip. Morning sunlight streamed in through the curtains. Outside the window a bird chirped a happy tune. Serena didn't feel at all happy. She felt overwhelmed.

After breakfast they'd sat down to fill in the multipaged application and realized they needed a photo to attach to the paperwork. So she'd put on one of the outfits she'd purchased, curled her hair with hot rollers to soften her look and applied a touch of makeup. Now she and Josh were posing in front of the camera, trying to appear the happy, loving couple they were pretending to be. Apparently it wasn't working.

With a twist of her lips, Serena scooted closer to Josh on the couch and tried to ignore the spicy fragrance of his aftershave as he leaned into her, but his scent swirled around her, teasing her senses. She involuntarily inhaled deeply, filling her lungs with the pleasing aroma, and her insides melted a little. His arm was draped casually around her shoulders, heavy, yet comforting. His hand rested lightly on her biceps. The pads of his fingertips traced little circles on her skin, creating pleasant shivers to cascade through her. Was he trying to relax her? If so, his tactic wasn't working.

It was a good thing she'd changed into another summery dress rather than her work suit because she was growing warmer by the minute. She had to force herself not to fan her hot face. She was sure her cheeks would be bright red in the photo.

"Smile, please," Linda coaxed.

Serena tried, but was sure the smile would appear forced.

Linda snapped several shots. She came out from behind the camera. "I think I got one we can work with."

"Wonderful," Josh said. His arm remained around Serena.

She turned to look at him, suddenly loath to move. She couldn't deny how nice it felt snuggled this close to him, to have his arm around her as if they really were a couple.

But they weren't a real couple. She couldn't lose herself in some crazy fantasy. This, the touching and looks, this entire masquerade was a job for a specific purpose. Forcing herself to stay on task, she said, "We have to write our statement. Would you do the honors?"

His eyebrows rose. "Me? Shouldn't the mother-to-be do it?"

Her breathing quickened as an unexpected yearning rocketed through her. Shaking her head at his teasing jab and at her reaction, she said, "We'll do it together, then."

They had already filled out most of the application as soon as they'd returned to the cover house. Besides the obvious details of who, what, where and how much they were worth, they'd each written short paragraphs on their hobbies, their interests and their talents, as well as their community involvements. Now they had to write a statement detailing why they wanted to adopt and how having a child would change their lives.

They'd agreed to put as much truth into their answers as possible. Serena had read Josh's and he read hers. She couldn't help but wonder what he thought about the fact that she collected teacups or that she attended a weekly Bible study when she was in town.

She hadn't known he liked to grow his own vegetables or that he served in a Christian church-sponsored soup kitchen during the holidays.

Realizing they shared a faith in God muddied her feelings about Josh.

On one hand she was glad to know Josh was a believer, yet she couldn't let that soften her anger toward him. He might profess to know Jesus, but having faith didn't absolve him of the blame in her brother's death.

Nothing would ever do that.

Because nothing would bring Daniel back.

She shrugged off Josh's arm and scooted away.

Hurt flashed in his eyes as he sat forward to pick up the pen. "Okay, we write it together."

She missed the weight of his arm. Stupid of her. And foolish, given their relationship would never be more than professional.

Over the next half hour they discussed, debated and finally came to a tentative agreement on why Mr. and Mrs. Andrews wanted to adopt and why they thought having a child would change the couple's lives for the better.

"You two work well together," Linda observed as she came into the room.

"Were you eavesdropping?" Serena teased.

Linda smiled. "I'll admit to a little eavesdropping now and then. I'm sure when Mrs. Munders comes here for her inspection she'll have questions for the Andrewses' live-in aunt."

"That is true," Josh said. "Would you mind glancing

over this application and making sure we didn't miss anything?"

"Of course." Linda laid out a printed copy of the photo she'd selected. "This is the best of the bunch."

Serena picked up the picture and stared at the image of Jack and Susan Andrews. They looked happy, healthy, in love. The perfect yuppie couple. But the relationship portrayed in the photo was just an illusion. A weird hollowness settled in her chest. What in the world was wrong with her? She set the photo back down.

Linda read through the application and declared it well done.

An hour later, with the application and photo in hand, Josh and Serena drove to the Perfect Family Adoption Agency. The receptionist ushered them right away into Mrs. Munders's office.

"Lovely," Mrs. Munders gushed as she looked over the application. "I see you both attend church."

Josh gathered Serena's hand in his. "Yes. We haven't yet found a place of worship here. We thought we'd get settled in a bit and then look for a church home."

Brilliant man. Serena squeezed his hand. He squeezed back.

"Wonderful. I believe our spiritual health is as important as our physical health."

"Do you and your husband attend a church?" Serena asked, curious how they could profess to have faith and yet be involved in the heinous crime of human trafficking.

"I do. My dear Fred is not so inclined," she said with a sad shake of her head.

I would think not, Serena thought sourly. But how could Mrs. Munders attend church, hear the word of God and still participate in something so evil?

Serena's grandmother's voice echoed in her head: *Judge not, lest ye be judged.*

Easier said than done. Serena adjusted her thoughts and tuned back in to what Mrs. Munders was saying.

"Everything seems to be in order." Mrs. Munders put the file in a drawer. "I'll have to do a little vetting, but I'm sure we'll be able to help you."

"That's good news," Serena said, affecting an excited yet desperate note to her voice.

Mrs. Munders steepled her hands on the desk. "Now, when would be a good time for a home visit?"

"The sooner the better," Josh said.

"Excellent." Mrs. Munders stared at them for a long moment, her gaze going out of focus, as if she'd become lost in her thoughts.

Serena shared a curious glance with Josh.

Josh cleared his throat. "Mrs. Munders?"

The older woman blinked. "Yes, dear?"

"We were discussing the home visit," Serena prompted.

Mrs. Munders made a silent *oh* with her mouth. "Right. A home visit. How would two days from now work? Say, ten in the morning?"

"Thursday would be perfect," Serena said.

"Since we're rushing this through, the home inspection will be lengthy. Normally I like to visit a couple's home at least three times before placing a child."

Serena suspected Mrs. Munders always had a "rushed placement," in which she somehow managed to place a stolen baby into the desperate adoptive parents' arms more quickly than usual. That would allow her to charge extra.

"We are grateful you are pushing through our adoption," Josh said. "When can we see the baby?"

The older woman waved her hand. "There'll be time for that later."

"It is an infant, right?" Serena asked.

"Oh, I almost forgot." Mrs. Munders opened a drawer

and pulled out a thick manila envelope. "This is the next step in the process."

"What is this?" Serena asked, taking the offered envelope.

"The dossier. A few more forms."

Glancing inside the envelope flap, Serena let out a silent whistle. A few was relative apparently to Mrs. Munders. There were at least fifty pages' worth of forms.

"Now there's the matter of the deposit," Mrs. Munders said.

"Didn't we already put money down for a deposit?" Serena asked, thinking about the five thousand dollars Josh paid Mrs. Munders on their first visit to the agency.

"That was the application fee, dear," Mrs. Munders said. "The deposit is for securing that you receive the next available child."

Josh frowned. "Doesn't the birth mother have some say in who the child goes to?"

"I thought you had an infant already in mind for us?" Serena said at the same time.

Mrs. Munders's gaze bounced between them then returned Josh's frown. "Of course. We give the poor dears choices from couples we've already deemed worthy. As soon as I process the application and the dossier I'll know if you're worthy."

There was so much wrong with the words coming out of Mrs. Munders's mouth that Serena's head spun. The evidence they'd collected showed the Munderses used coercion and intimidation to secure children. Choice had nothing to do with it.

They'd been informed of this by Morgan Smith, a missionary to Mexico who'd revealed that many of the children being taken out of Mexico and brought to the United States were in fact being forcibly removed from their mothers. Morgan almost paid with her life for sharing this with the authorities. Serena wondered how many other mothers in other countries around the world were having their babies ripped from their arms. The Munderses and their cohorts had proven they would stop at nothing to keep their dirty secret safe.

Serena's fingers tightened around Josh's.

"I assume we'll have to sign a contract," Josh said, diverting the conversation. "Will Mr. Munders draw that up? I understand he is a lawyer."

"Yes, Fred will draw up a contract once we have a child ready to hand over to you," Mrs. Munders said, clearly unperturbed by the fact they had done their own vetting.

Serena cocked her head. "You told Jack you had an infant that needed placing," she pressed, not satisfied with Mrs. Munders's earlier implication that they had to be "worthy" of adopting. "You said we could have a child by the end of the week."

The blank expression in Mrs. Munders's gaze didn't bode well.

"Did I?" Mrs. Munders opened her ledger and traced her finger down one of the columns. "Oh, yes, I might. Though the child in question will be closer to nine months old. Will that be a problem?"

Serena's heart lurched. Baby Kay? She'd be nine months old by now. If she wasn't already with a family, where were the Munderses keeping her? "Where is the baby now?"

"Baby? Oh, goodness, I don't have a baby. I mean I did once when I was young, but I'm too old now." Mrs. Munders laughed softly. "Though I suppose Sarah thought she was too old, too…." She stared off at something unseen.

Was she really comparing herself to Sarah from the Bible? Serena's blood boiled. She fought to not judge the older woman, but it was hard not to, given all Serena knew about Fred and Matilda Munders and their illegal activities.

After a heartbeat, Serena snapped, "Mrs. Munders."

Mrs. Munders's expression cleared. "You wanted a baby." She consulted her ledger again. "Hmm. Yes. You could have a baby by the end of the month."

Serena blew out a frustrated breath.

Beside her, Josh stiffened. "You said by the end of the week."

"Oh, goodness." Mrs. Munders waved a hand. "That would be pushing it. I'll see what I can do." Her gaze turned shrewd. "Two hundred thousand."

"Excuse me?" Josh's voice held a note of disbelief. "That's the deposit?"

Glad Josh was able to follow the woman's conversational gymnastics, Serena swallowed. "That's a lot of money."

No wonder the Munderses were willing to risk the penalties of operating their illegal adoption scam. With income like that coming from the hundreds of adoptions that Mrs. Munders boasted of, they had to be rolling in dough.

Forcing back the simmering anger, Serena clamped her jaw tight before she let loose with a tirade against the Munderses and the evil they'd inflicted on innocent people.

Mrs. Munders blinked. Frowned. Then shook her head. "Oh, no, dear. The deposit is one-fourth of the estimated cost. Fifty thousand. The rest can be paid out on an installment plan."

That was an exorbitant amount of money no matter how you looked at it.

"I'd like to meet Mr. Munders and review the contract before we hand over any more money," Josh stated in a hard, unyielding voice. The voice he used when dealing with criminals.

Serena gave his hand a squeeze as a warning not to

be too harsh. He'd been worried about her blowing it; he could just as easily if he came on too strong.

Mrs. Munders gave him a patient smile. "All in good time, dear. Fred is a busy man." She held out her hand as if she expected them to have that kind of cash tucked away in Serena's purse or Josh's wallet. "The deposit, please?"

Josh stood, tugging Serena to her feet. "As I said, not until I review the contract."

Serena threw him a stunned glance. Had he just scrubbed this assignment? She had to do something to keep their fish from getting away. Infusing into her voice the panic fluttering in her stomach, Serena said, "Please, Mrs. Munders, I'm desperate for a baby. Please help us."

The compassion filling the older woman's gaze couldn't be fake, could it?

"I'll do my best to arrange a meeting for you with Fred," Mrs. Munders said. "I have every confidence you'll be a mother soon. Until then, I'll continue with the vetting process."

"You'll still come to our house on Thursday morning, correct?" Josh asked.

"Yes. I'll be there."

As soon as they were in the SUV and heading back to their cover house, Josh slammed his palm against the steering wheel. "This whole thing is driving me insane."

Serena felt the same frustration course through her veins. "There's something wrong with Mrs. Munders."

"You think?" The sarcasm dripping from his words could fill a bucket.

"No need for you to get nasty with me," Serena snapped.

He exhaled noisily. "Sorry. It's just…"

"I know." She'd never seen Josh get this riled before. For six months they'd been doggedly following leads and clues only to fall short of putting together a firm case against the Munderses. Because someone within the Marshals Service was clueing the bad guys in and keeping the marshals from doing their job. But not this time.

They were taking precautions, keeping this assignment so tight to the vest that there was no way the betrayer could interfere. "We have to be patient. We've got this. We're close to obtaining the solid evidence we need to bring the Munderses down. Have some faith."

He glanced at her. "You constantly surprise me."

"What?"

"You always seem to know what I need. Thank you for the pep talk." He rolled his shoulders. "Teacups?"

So he had noticed. Wistfulness filled her. "It was something my mother started when I was a young girl. Every Sunday afternoon we'd have tea parties while Dad and Daniel had their 'boy' time. Every once in a while Mom would surprise me with a new teacup." She shrugged, hoping to cover the sentiment behind her words. "Now whenever I see a teacup I like, I buy it."

"How long has it been since you've seen your mom?"

"Daniel's funeral." Serena stared out the window at the passing cityscape. The Gateway Arch drew her gaze, its bright silver steel gleaming in the summer sun. "Of course, she and Dad had a fight." Her throat constricted.

Josh threaded his fingers through hers. Startled, she jerked her gaze to him.

"Daniel told me how awful your parents' fights could get."

"Did he?" She wasn't surprised. Daniel had thought of Josh as a brother.

They'd been best friends as well as coworkers. She'd never had a relationship like that with anyone but Daniel.

She stared at her fingers, entwined with Josh's. His hand was so much bigger and stronger than hers. She knew she should draw away from him. There was no reason for him to be holding her hand when they had no audience for their performance as Susan and Jack Andrews.

Certainly there was no reason for her to be hanging on as if she was afraid she'd fly away on a gust of grief. Still, she allowed their hands to remain exactly as they were, unable to break the connection.

And she had no idea why.

Josh's cell phone rang.

Telling herself she was relieved, she slipped her hand away. "Want me to get that?"

"Please. It's my personal cell." He took the phone out of his suit pocket and handed it to her.

She pushed the answer button. "Josh's phone."

"Summers, it's Harrison."

"Hello, sir." She pressed the speaker button. "I have you on speaker. Josh is driving."

"Good. Head to the airport. You're flying to Minneapolis. We found Lonnie, Baby Kay's mother. I want her in protective custody now."

"She could be the one to link all the pieces together."

The intensity in Serena's voice reverberated through Josh. At the stoplight, he glanced at her. His gaze snagged on the slender lines of her neck below the soft curls of her auburn hair, distracting him for a moment from her comment.

She appeared comfortable in the pretty dress she'd worn to see Mrs. Munders. She looked appealing, carefree and so much more relaxed and less repressed in the casual clothing and sandals. Not so angry with him. Of course he could be imagining the softening.

But…she'd given him that pep talk about the case, whereas before she might have condemned him, saying he was getting what he deserved.

Which he still deserved. She had every right to be angry with him. He was angry with himself.

He turned back to the road in time to see the light change to green. He stepped on the accelerator. "Lonnie's in danger. We need to bring her in and get her somewhere safe."

"That's for sure."

The road congestion would make the fourteen-plus-mile drive to the Lambert–St. Louis International Airport take longer than it should.

Despite the powder-blue sky overhead and the fresh air swirling through the open windows, anxiety knotted in Josh's chest. He'd removed his suit jacket and loosened his tie, but he was still uneasy. Lonnie and her baby had been targeted once, and Baby Kay had been kidnapped. The people responsible might believe Lonnie could identify them.

"It will be interesting to hear her story," Serena said. "What possessed her to leave her baby with Emma Bullock?"

"We'll know soon enough."

Serena flipped on the radio. The newscaster talked about Missouri congressman Peter Simms's upcoming appearance in St. Louis. Rumor was the state's golden boy would be announcing his bid for the presidency.

Josh glanced in the rearview mirror and noticed a white van two cars back. He couldn't see the license plate, so he couldn't be sure it was the same van that had escaped from the warehouse yesterday. But his gut told him something was up. To get a handle on the situation, he changed lanes quickly. So did the van.

"We have a tail," he stated calmly. They'd been through this drill numerous times in the course of this investigation. "The white van two cars back."

Serena twisted in her seat to look out the rear window.

"Call SLMPD," Josh instructed as he picked up speed.

"On it." She made the call and gave the police dispatcher their location.

Josh turned down a side street that he knew had one way in and out, hoping to trap the van between them and the police.

The van continued straight, whizzing past like a cloud.

"Guess you were wrong," Serena said softly without any censure.

Unease tickled the fine hairs at the base of Josh's neck. He hadn't thought so, but maybe...

He went around the block and rejoined the flow of traffic. Up ahead the light turned red. He brought the vehicle to a halt, his gaze searching the area, checking the rearview mirror. Nothing. The white van had disappeared.

The light changed. He stepped on the gas. Halfway through the intersection a flash of movement in his peripheral vision jerked his gaze to the left. The white van ran the red light in the cross traffic and sped toward them.

With his heart in his throat, Josh floored it. But he was a moment too late.

The van struck the SUV, sending the vehicle spinning. The sickening thud, crunch and squeal of metal on metal and the tinkling of shattering glass mingled with Serena's scream echoed inside Josh's head.

Fearing for Serena, he reached out a hand, trying desperately to save her from the impact.

SEVEN

The world spun. Or was it only inside her head? Serena blinked, trying to focus, but her head hurt as if someone had mistaken her for a block of ice and was repeatedly stabbing the sharp tip of an ice pick into her brain. She felt the blows all the way to her bones.

Aches and pains screamed from various points all over her body. The seat belt pressed across her chest, pinning her to the seat. An acrid chemical smell made her gag, and a fine dust filled her nostrils. The deflated air bag lay in her lap.

A moan sounded on her left. Josh!

Alarm pummeled her insides. She dragged her gaze to him. He held his head in his hands. The steering wheel air bag lay in a clump across his thigh. She touched his shoulder. "Are you all right?"

He lifted his head and met her gaze. His nose dripped blood, and his cheeks were red and abraded. "Yeah, you?"

"I'll live," she said, thankful for that fact.

They'd been broadsided. She remembered seeing the grille of the van bearing down on them, and then the horrible sounds of the crash and the vehicle spinning. Thankfully, she'd had her seat far enough back that she hadn't been hit in the face with the dashboard as the air bag deployed. She sent up a silent prayer of thanks.

Sirens punctuated the air. An ambulance roared to a halt a few feet away, followed by a police cruiser and a fire truck. Heroes to the rescue. She tried to smile but it turned into a wince.

The paramedics removed them from the wreckage and checked them over.

"It's a wonder you both aren't hurt more seriously," the EMT said as she put her gear away.

"Not a wonder—a blessing," Serena replied. Every muscle ached as she rose and stretched, but she pushed through the pain. She would not show any weakness.

She glanced at Josh. The paramedic had given him an ice pack to put on his nose.

He winced when he stood. "Thank you."

Moving closer to him, Serena had to force herself to refrain from touching him to assure herself that he was all right.

His smile peeked out from behind the ice pack. "Nothing broken."

"I'm glad," she replied, meaning it.

Tipping his chin toward the officers milling around the crash site, he said, "Let's see what they've found."

Josh introduced them by their cover names. Serena knew their boss would square away the accident report once the undercover assignment was finished.

The police officer acknowledged the introduction with a nod. "Witnesses saw the van whip a U-turn and pull to the curb, where he sat idling. When you entered the intersection the van shot forward to run the red light and headed on a collision course straight for you."

"I saw it out of the corner of my eye," Josh said. "I floored it, hoping it would go past us."

"From all accounts it was aiming for you," the officer said. "Witnesses say the driver bailed out at the last second, rolled a few feet and then jumped up and ran down the street, and disappeared."

"Figures," Serena muttered. How had the guy found them?

Josh thanked the officers, then cupped Serena's elbow and propelled her into the shadow of a building. "I'll call the chief. He'll want to know what's happened."

Serena leaned against the side of the building, her gaze alert for any signs of the man who'd tried to kill them.

Josh hung up. "The chief is on his way. He'll take us back to the house."

They didn't have to wait long. Chief Harrison pulled to the curb in his personal vehicle, a hatchback coupe.

Lines of worry bracketed his blue eyes. "You two okay?"

"A little banged up," Josh said.

"Unfortunately the BMW didn't fare as well," Serena said.

The chief waved a dismissive hand. "I don't care about the vehicle."

"What about Lonnie?" Serena asked. "If the leak in our department finds out she's been found…"

"I called in Colton Phillips. He and FBI agent Lisette Sutton are headed to Minnesota. They'll escort Miss Bogler here. Once she arrives I want you two to interview her."

"Good idea, sir," Josh said. "Colton can be trusted. He proved himself with the Baby C case."

They'd met U.S. marshal Colton Phillips a few months back when he'd been moved to the Denver office. He had been instrumental in rescuing a baby from the clutches of an unscrupulous criminal who later escaped and disappeared. The baby, dubbed Baby C by the marshals, was reunited with her mother when Dylan McIntyre had come forward with information about Munders's illegal adoption scheme. Unfortunately all the incriminating evidence provided by McIntyre had disappeared from the marshals' office. Which was why Serena and Josh needed to keep their current assignment under tight wraps.

"Where are we on Operation: Undercover Marriage?" the chief asked as he signaled to change lanes.

Serena's lips twisted with wry amusement. She remembered how irritated she'd been when this assignment started. Now…she wasn't sure how she felt. Which was weird for her. She was usually pretty cut and dried.

Josh gave the chief a verbal report.

"You're making good progress," the chief said. "But we need to speed things up. Can you push a little harder?"

"We will, sir," Josh promised.

Serena wasn't sure the promise would yield much in the way of results. Mrs. Munders seemed to move at her own pace. Getting her to move quickly might prove difficult. "Sir, Mrs. Munders exhibits some strange behavior patterns."

"Like?"

"Mistaking me for her dead daughter. Forgetting the topic of conversation midsentence. Staring off into space."

"It's becoming harder to imagine she's the mastermind behind the illegal adoptions," Josh chimed in.

"Her husband?"

"According to Dylan McIntyre, Fred Munders is probably knee-deep into the illegal activities. The judge who signed off on the adoptions was investigated, but there wasn't anything to suggest he was involved," Josh stated. "But as for the mastermind…the man they call 'Mr. Big'…" He shrugged. "We won't know until we have enough evidence to arrest the Munderses and question them."

The chief's gaze met Serena's in the rearview mirror.

"What has Linda been able to discover from the photos you took?"

Frustration bubbled. Serena had hoped the pictures would be helpful. "Last we talked, the ledger was undecipherable. Some sort of shorthand code known only to Mrs. Munders. As for the photo gallery of babies, Linda's been running them through facial recognition to see if any pop with missing person's reports. So far nothing. We're also keeping an eye out for a baby with a mark on her cheek."

Emma had said the baby Lonnie had given her to hold—she remembered the child's name was Kay—had a small square strawberry mark on her cheek.

Harrison drummed his fingers on the steering wheel. "And the neighbor family with adopted children?"

"We'll be meeting them on Saturday," Josh answered. "So far they check out. They adopted their kids through a different organization. One with a stellar reputation."

"Mrs. Munders is coming to the cover house for a home inspection," Josh said. "As part of the adoption process."

"I want to thank you both for taking on this assignment," Harrison said as he stopped the car in the driveway of the cover house. "I don't know who else in the department I can trust right now."

A rush of anger swept through Serena.

Any of the dozen or so people in the St. Louis office could be the one working for the bad guys. Serena hoped it would be only a matter of time before she and Josh brought them to justice.

The doorbell chime filled the house and sent Josh's heart into overdrive. He glanced at the clock. Mrs. Munders was right on time for their home inspection.

Linda wiped her hands on the apron tied around her

waist. "I'll answer the door." She marched out of the kitchen as if she was about to do battle.

He slid off the barstool in the kitchen and held out his hand to Serena. "Here we go."

She hesitated a second before slipping her hand into his. Her shoulders were hiked to her ears.

"I don't know why I'm so nervous." She let out a stiff laugh. "It's not like I'm really concerned what she thinks of our home."

Our home. Josh liked the sound of that way more than he should. Over the past day and a half they'd done everything they could think of to prepare for Mrs. Munders's visit. Even going so far as having a mock wedding photo taken.

Linda had visited a local thrift store and bought a wedding gown for Serena. Josh had worn the tux he kept for formal occasions. Using her high-tech camera and Photoshop, Linda created a realistic-looking picture of Josh and Serena posing on the steps of a white-steepled church. She'd then blown up the photo, framed it and hung it in the entryway.

Every time Josh passed the image his heart did a little double take, and he had to remind himself it was all a charade.

But hidden inside, in a place he tried to ignore, was the longing for this all to be real. He longed for a loving wife, for a normal, healthy marriage. To raise a family.

To wipe away the torment of his own childhood and do better than his father ever had.

Maybe it was the fake photo or the way they'd been together these past few days, but he could easily imagine Serena in that role. He could imagine working together during the day and coming home together at night.

Whoa! Back the bus up. What was he thinking?

Clearly he wasn't. At least not rationally.

Mentally taming his wild thoughts, he forced his focus onto the woman at his side. Serena bit at her lip. Tender affection flooded him. He tucked her hand in the crook of his elbow. "Hey. Don't worry. Nerves will lend credibility to our cover."

"Right." She squared her shoulders, let out a breath and plastered a smile on her face. "Here we go."

They found Linda and Mrs. Munders seated on the sofa in the living room.

"Mrs. Munders, welcome to our home," Serena said, gliding forward to take the older woman's hand. "I see you've met Jack's aunt Linda."

Josh marveled at the transformation. No one would have guessed moments before Serena had been a nervous mess. Now she appeared confident and hospitable. His admiration and respect for her grew.

"Indeed I have." Mrs. Munders patted Serena's hand. "Hello, Jack. You look well."

"As do you, Mrs. Munders." He and Serena sat on the love seat and faced the two women.

"Can I offer you something to drink?" Linda asked.

"No, no. I'm sure you're all anxious to get this over with." Mrs. Munders pushed to her feet. She swayed for a moment.

Serena jumped up and held on to Mrs. Munders elbow. "Are you okay?"

"Yes, dear. Must be the heat."

Josh didn't think it was warm in the house. The air-conditioning was pumping out cool air, keeping the house at a comfortable temperature.

After a tour of the house and yard, Mrs. Munders closed her notebook with a satisfied snap. "All seems in order. I love your plans for a backyard play structure. Children need plenty of time outdoors away from electronics." She tsked. "Life is so different today with all the gadgets that keep kids occupied. You'll need to get your nursery in order soon."

"So you have a baby for us?" Serena asked. "A girl or boy? How soon could we meet the birth mother?"

Mrs. Munders held up a hand. "Soon. Very soon. We don't know the gender yet."

Serena frowned. "But earlier it seemed you had a specific baby in mind. One that was nine months old."

Mrs. Munders cocked her head and blinked at her, and then without replying to Serena's statement, turned her sharp-eyed gaze on Josh. "I relayed your desire to meet with Fred, but he is extremely busy at the moment, so you'll just have to be content to deal with me on the deposit."

If he gave her the money they might never have an excuse to meet Fred. "I'm sure Mr. Munders could make some time for us. Money's not an issue. However, I do need to look over the contract before making a payment."

Mrs. Munders breathed in, her nostrils flaring. "Well, I will explain this to Fred. However, waiting on him might put a crimp in how soon we can give you a child."

"You'll talk to your husband, though?" Serena said, her voice rising slightly with the appropriate amount of desperation.

"Yes, dear." She consulted her notebook. "I will need to come back next week."

"But you said you'd have a baby for us by the end of this week," Josh said, his voice hard.

"Without the deposit…" She shrugged. "You understand how it is. We must be paid up front before we can proceed."

"Fine. I'll give you half the deposit now and the other half when I can meet face-to-face with Mr. Munders and review the contract," Josh stated.

"I'll get the check," Serena said and hurried away.

"She's a sweet girl," Mrs. Munders said into the awkward silence.

"Yes, Susan is a gem," Josh replied.

Serena returned with the check in hand. She gave it to Mrs. Munders but held on for a moment. "Please. You'll find me a baby."

"Of course, dear. You can count on me." Mrs. Munders pocketed the money and left.

"Now what?" Serena asked, leaning against the closed door. "We just wait for her to decide we're desperate enough to pay the rest of the money?"

Waiting was never one of Josh's strong suits. "I'm calling Fred Munders. This cat-and-mouse game is already old."

Serena pushed off the door. "I know the chief said to push, but what if we spook Fred?"

"I'm willing to take that chance." Josh hoped she'd support him in this, but chances were she wouldn't. She'd made it clear she didn't trust him. He doubted she'd trust his judgment, either. A twinge of hurt made him hesitate. Disgusted with this sudden need for her approval, he took out his cell phone. But he couldn't dial the number. Frustrated he looked at her, waiting for a reaction.

Slowly, she gave an approving nod. "Make the call."

Gratified by the encouragement way more than he should have been, he made the call only to be told by the answering service that Munders was out of the office and would return his call on Monday.

"If he doesn't call by the end of the day on Monday, I'll call again," Josh vowed.

Linda stepped out of the kitchen. "I just talked to the chief. Marshal Phillips has Lonnie Bogler in protective custody. They are driving here from Minnesota. Apparently Lonnie has a phobia of flying, so they rented a car. They should arrive in St. Louis by Sunday afternoon."

"Until then we continue to do what we can to locate our friend in the white van and find Baby Kay," Serena said, her voice brisk. She headed toward the downstairs den, leaving Josh and Linda in the entryway.

"You two seem to be getting along better," Linda observed.

They were settling into a more cohesive rhythm. Fondness for his pretend wife spread through his chest. "Yes, whatever you said to her the other day worked," Josh said, grateful that Serena was trying so hard.

Linda smiled. Her gaze drifted to the fake wedding portrait hanging on the wall. "You two make a good team."

"Maybe." But he had a feeling once this assignment was over, Serena would prefer not working with him again. He would miss seeing her every day and hearing her voice. He would miss the way she challenged him and inspired him.

But that was the way it would have to be. And then he could go back to feeling guilty all by himself.

Saturday afternoon was sunny and humid. Serena put on another summery dress and sandals. She had to admit she was grateful for the flowing material in this mid-June heat wave scorching St. Louis. Of course, she thought, it could be nerves making her temperature rise.

That or her attraction to Josh that sizzled below the surface. An attraction she was struggling to control.

She smoothed a hand over her skirt to calm the quaking of her knees, as Josh slipped an arm around her waist and propelled her out of the air-conditioned house.

She, Josh and Linda joined the neighbors in the street. Tables were set up with umbrellas to provide shade, and several barbecues gleamed in the sun with men in golf shirts wearing the occasional "Kiss the Cook" aprons attending to delicious-smelling meats simmering on the grill.

Trina introduced them down the line. Serena memorized the names and faces, smiling with interest as she played the role of Susan Andrews, answering questions about her and "Jack" and asking general questions of her own. Several families with children as well as older retired couples closer to Linda's age mingled about.

When Serena met the Frellner family, she immediately hit it off with Joyce Frellner. She was a robust woman with a big laugh and obviously a big heart, judging by the passel of kids following her around. There was two-year-old Kate, a dark-skinned little beauty adopted from India, and Gerard and Marie, five-year-old twins adopted from Korea. Blake, ten, and Cindy, twelve, were the Frellners' biological children.

Taking a seat at one of the tables next to Joyce, Serena said, "We're in the process of adopting."

"How wonderful," Joyce beamed. "You won't regret it. What agency are you working through?"

"Perfect Family Adoption."

Joyce made a face. Beside her, her husband, Thomas, whistled. "That will set you back a pretty penny."

"You've worked with Perfect Family?" Josh asked as he stepped up behind Serena's chair, his hands settling on her shoulders.

A river of sensation washed over Serena. She fought the urge to squirm out of his reach. "Susan" would welcome her husband's touch. With that in mind, she reached up to pat Josh's hand, loving the feel of his strong fingers firm against her skin.

"We tried, but they wanted way too much money," Joyce said. "The other agencies we looked into didn't have nearly the fees that Perfect Family did."

"Perfect Family deals mostly with domestic adoptions," Thomas stated.

"I'd heard they also handled adoptions from Mexico and Europe," Josh said.

Thomas shrugged. "That could be."

"Did you meet Mr. and Mrs. Munders?" Serena asked.

Joyce picked up Kate and bounced her on her knee. "Mrs. Munders. She seemed nice enough."

A tall man with a head of silver hair carried a pitcher of lemonade to the table. "Munders?"

"Hi, Bill." Thomas stood to shake the man's hand. "These are the new neighbors who moved into the Zanettis' house. Jack and Susan Andrews."

Josh shook Bill's hand. "We were discussing the Perfect Family Adoption Agency. It's owned by Fred and Matilda Munders."

"I went to law school with Fred," Bill said, pulling up a chair.

"You know the Munderses?" Serena was eager to hear what the man had to say. "So you're a lawyer, as well?"

"Retired state's prosecutor."

Josh's hand tightened slightly on Serena's shoulder. "What can you tell us about Fred Munders?"

Bill's eyebrows hiked up. "Not much. I haven't seen him in years. He has a mean poker face."

"So that's what you were doing all those nights when you were supposed to be at the library studying," a slender woman with blond hair and blue eyes said as she joined them. "I always wondered."

Bill took his wife's hand. "Not every time. Besides, many alliances were made at those poker games."

"Alliances?" Josh said.

With a dry laugh, Bill explained, "We all had ambitions. Some grander than others. Fred went into private practice. I went into the D.A.'s office. Another buddy,

Simon, became a judge and another went into international law. Larry now lives in Switzerland."

Serena reached up to grab Josh's hand. "Judge Simon Simms?" The judge who'd signed off on the illegal adoptions coming out of Mexico that Dylan McIntyre had put together for Munders.

Bud and Burke had checked into the judge at the time, but found nothing to suggest he was involved. The conclusion the office had come to after looking into the judge was he'd been acting in good faith since the documents McIntyre had drawn up for the adoptions had appeared legit.

"Yes, do you know Simon?"

"No," Josh answered smoothly. "He's Congressman Peter Simms's brother, right?"

Bill nodded. "Peter is a few years younger than Simon. I've only met Peter a handful of times."

"I heard he's throwing his hat in the ring for the presidency," Thomas said. "What do you think of that?"

"From what I know of him he's competent and smooth. A typical politician," Bill answered, his tone neutral. "No better or worse than the one already in place."

"Hamburgers are ready!" one of the men at the grill called out.

Everyone left the table except for Josh and Serena. He held out his hand and pulled her to her feet. Tugging her close, he leaned in to whisper, "We need to take another look at the Simms brothers."

"This could be the break we've been waiting for."

Trina waved to them. "Come on, you two lovebirds. Get your food while it's hot."

Josh grinned. "Lovebirds."

Serena's face flamed. "She thinks we're kissing."

A playful gleam entered his brown eyes. "I wouldn't want to disappoint."

His head dipped and his lips captured hers for a kiss that stole her breath and weakened her knees.

Splaying her hands on the hard plane of his chest, she meant to push him away but instead surprised herself by curling her fingers to grasp the fabric of his polo shirt and tug him closer.

He gave a low murmur of surprise and pleasure.

A soft chuckle to their right brought Serena to her senses. She jerked back, and was thankful for Josh's strong arms keeping her upright. He'd kissed her for show, but she'd forgotten they were onstage. Mortification burned in her cheeks.

Linda laid her plate on the table beside them. "Oh, don't mind me. Carry on."

Josh's deep laugh rumbled from his chest as he stepped back, releasing his hold on Serena. She missed his arms around her. Wanted to do as Linda suggested and carry on. But that wouldn't be wise. This was all pretend, but that kiss…that didn't feel at all fake.

EIGHT

The last of the sun's glow disappeared over the horizon and day turned to night. A temperature drop brought welcome relief from the heat of the summer day.

Surprised by the camaraderie and contentment filling him, Josh sat with some of the neighborhood men talking sports and golf averages, but his gaze kept straying to Serena. His beautiful pretend wife.

She sat with the women, her arms full of little Kate Frellner. Serena held the child so comfortably, as if she was born to be a mother. So different from the gun-wielding, door-kicking, top-notch marshal he'd come to rely on as his partner.

Seeing her like this created an ache deep in his heart. Despite how real and right kissing her had felt, how natural and intimate their relationship had seemed throughout the day, Josh couldn't forget this was all fictitious.

He was as dumb as a box of rocks to let Serena get so close. Because deep down inside he knew that if he fell for her, it would change his world. He would never be able to just be her coworker. He would want it all: her love, marriage, the house and kids. He'd want the life they were fabricating. A life that would come with too high a price. He couldn't risk it. Couldn't risk what it would take to have it all. It would be better for them both if he shut down his heart altogether.

But he couldn't do that and be a convincing husband.

He wished Daniel were here. He'd know how to handle this. From the moment they'd met, Daniel had been the voice of reason in Josh's life. With him gone, Josh was having to rely on his own judgment and logic. Which he didn't question when it came to the job. But in regards to Serena? He was floundering.

The party started to break up. Families said good-night and drifted off to their homes. Linda had long since retired. Josh helped Trina's husband, Darrell, put the tables and chairs back in their garage. Josh was loath for the evening to end. The wall between him and Serena would go back up when they weren't onstage.

As much as he knew that was what should happen, what would be the best thing for them professionally and emotionally, he did not want to go backward when seeing her with the kids tonight, kissing her, having her by his side was chipping away at his need to stay detached.

"You and Susan should join us for a round of golf tomorrow after church," Darrell said as they walked out to the sidewalk where Serena and Trina stood talking.

"I'll speak to my wife." The words rolled off his tongue with such ease. Alarm bells clanged in his head. He wanted to call Serena his wife in real life. But that wasn't possible. He had to get a grip. She might have thawed some toward him, but his guilt over Daniel's death would never allow him to find happiness. Especially not with the sister of that man he'd let down.

When he reached Serena's side, she took his hand. His heart squeezed with tight longing and regret for what could never be as their fingers folded over each other.

"Trina invited us to attend their church with them in the morning." The excitement in Serena's eyes tugged at him. Though it had been a while since he'd attended a formal service, he would go to please her.

He sucked in a breath but felt as if he was choking as realization slammed into him with the force of a baseball bat. He would do anything for her. Anything she asked. Which didn't bode well if he wanted to stay detached and unemotionally invested.

"That'd be great," he answered, hoping no one heard the strangled tone to his voice. He couldn't have Serena guess his feelings for her were changing…deepening. "And Darrell invited us to go golfing with them in the afternoon."

Serena laughed, the sound soft and alluring. "I've never golfed."

"The club offers lessons," Trina said. "Of course you'd have to join. We could sponsor you."

"That would be nice," Serena said. "Thank you. We'll talk about it."

Darrell put his arm around Trina. "Come on, hon, I want to catch the last of the Cardinals game."

The couple said good-night, and then retreated to their house. Josh and Serena stayed on the sidewalk for a moment, their fingers entwined. The sounds of night surrounding them like a symphony. The call of a whip-poor-will was answered by the hoot of an owl. An unseen animal rustled in the bushes. The racket of a cricket frog competed with a cicada, setting an irregular rhythm to the night, to his heartbeat.

"It's peaceful here," Serena said. "A good place to raise a family."

His pulse spiked. Yearning pierced him. He wanted what he'd been denied growing up. A normal, functional family. "Yes."

His voice sounded more like a croak.

"Trina was asking me about your background." She

turned her gaze to him. "I realized I don't know that much about your real background, other than you were born in Arkansas."

"Yep. In Lamar, population sixteen hundred." He couldn't keep the bitterness from creeping into his voice.

"Daniel said your father had passed on when you were young."

Josh stiffened. He didn't talk about his father. That was a subject better left swept under the rug. "Yes."

"I'm sorry. That must have been hard on you and your mom."

He let out a humorless laugh. "You have no idea."

She tilted her head to the side and peered at him as if he were a puzzle she needed to solve. "Does your mother still live in the house you grew up in?"

"No. Mom and I moved to Naples, Florida, after..." He couldn't finish the thought let alone say the words. He kept his past private. The pain was too hurtful, too raw, even after all these years. He'd opened up to Daniel because Daniel wouldn't let it go; he'd kept pushing until Josh had spilled the story. Josh sent up a silent plea that Serena wouldn't be as tenacious.

"How did your dad die?"

He took a step forward. "We should go in."

She held fast to his hand, rooting him in place. "Hey, wait. What's wrong?"

He faced the house, afraid to look at her, afraid that even in the muted light coming from the streetlamp she'd see the pain he fought to quell. "Discussing my past won't get this job done."

She released his hand and moved to stand in front of him. "Maybe not, but I'd like to know who I'm putting my trust in."

His breath caught. Did she trust him? He had to be sure, but his heart hammered in his chest, afraid to hope.

Could he hope she might forgive him, even though he could never forgive himself? "But are you putting your trust in me, Serena? Can you let go of what happened to your brother? I know I can't."

She looked away for a moment and took in a shuddering breath. When her gaze swung back to him, the shadows cast by the streetlamp hid her eyes. "I'm trying to."

That was progress, at least. Though he wasn't sure if he was relieved or more scared by the possibilities of what that could bring.

"Thank you for your honesty." He scrubbed a hand over his jaw, the bristles of his beard scraping his skin like this conversation was scraping his soul. "I failed Daniel. I won't fail you. I promise."

Her mouth quivered. "I'd like to believe that."

Doubt dripped from her words like drops of poison to his soul. Daniel's murder would always stand between them, a barrier that could never be breached.

The door to the house opened. Linda stepped out onto the porch and waved them in.

Thankful to have a reprieve from the conversation and the tide of rising guilt building inside of him, Josh tugged Serena up the stairs.

"I think I have something." There was no mistaking the excitement in Linda's voice.

They followed her to the den, their hands entwined. Josh savored the feel of her smooth palm encased in his. Savored the connection building between them, if only for these precious moments.

"Don't keep us in suspense—what is it?" Serena asked, letting go of Josh's hand to stand next to Linda at the desk.

The loss of her touch ached clear to his marrow.

"This." Linda held up a photo. "It's from the picture you snapped of the baby collage in Mrs. Munders's office."

Josh peered over Serena's shoulder. The fresh flowery scent of her shampoo clung to her hair and teased his senses. The photo in her hand was of a smiling, dark-haired woman holding a baby in her arms. "Okay. What are we looking at?"

Linda held out a magnifying glass. "Look at the baby's cheek."

Serena held the glass over the baby's face. She sucked in a noisy breath. Surprise washed over Josh. "A strawberry mark."

"Just like Emma described." Serena's enthusiasm brightened her face. "We just found Baby Kay."

"Who's the woman?" Josh asked, his gaze going to Linda.

"I'm running her image through facial recognition. If she's in any national database, we'll find her."

"She has to have a driver's license somewhere in the U.S., right?" Josh said.

"Hopefully," Linda replied. "But she could be in another country for all we know."

"We could ask Mrs. Munders," Serena said, setting the photo on the desk.

"If we don't have this woman's ID by Monday morning, we'll go to Perfect Family and find out who she is and where she has Baby Kay."

"And reunite Lonnie with her child."

"That, too." The hope in Serena's face spread through Josh like sunshine on a cold winter day. He hoped she wouldn't be disappointed. Lonnie had handed over her child to Emma and never returned. Yes, the young girl had been afraid, according to Emma, but why would she take off like that and trust her baby to a complete stranger? They wouldn't know the whole story until they had Lonnie in front of them.

Serena touched his arm. "Walk me to my room?"

His pulse jumped. Not once in the past six nights had

she made such an invitation. An anxious chord threaded
through him. For a heartbeat, he wondered if this request
had anything to do with the kiss they'd shared earlier, and
he just as quickly dismissed the idea. No, it was a precur-
sor to more questions about his past, questions he didn't
want to face. He'd have to keep her distracted, not allow
her an opportunity to probe into his past.

An unexpected smiled formed. "Sure, I'll walk you
to your room."

Her gaze narrowed as if she could read his thoughts.
He met her gaze steadily, daring her to call him on whatever was going on in that sharp mind of hers.

However, she didn't say a word but turned on her san-
daled heels and headed up the stairs. He followed, enjoy-
ing the way the hem of her skirt flirted with her knees.
She had well-defined calves, slim ankles.

As she drew to a halt at the end of the hall just shy of
the door to her room, she pivoted and said, "We were interrupted earlier. You never answered my question. What
happened to your father?"

Intent on distracting her, he reached out to tuck a lock
of her auburn hair behind her ear. "You should wear
dresses more often. You have great legs."

Her eyes widened. Even in the dim light of the hall he
could see the blush staining her cheeks. "Thank you. How
old were you when your father passed?"

Placing a hand on the wall beside her head, he said,
"Twelve. I like your hair this color." With his free hand
he ran his fingers through the strands skimming her jawline. Her hair was soft and silky.

She swallowed and pressed her back against the wall.
"That's young. Was he ill?"

He shrugged. "No." He wound a clump of her hair
around his finger and tugged her close. "I enjoyed spending time with you today. We were convincing." So much

so that he'd even had a hard time not believing she cared for him.

"Me, too. With you. We were," she squeaked. "If he wasn't ill, then how did he die?"

Closing the gap between them until his mouth hovered over hers, he whispered, "I'm going to kiss you."

Their gazes locked. Yearning flared in her eyes. This may have started out as a strategic tactic, a way to keep her questions at bay, but the longing streaming through his veins made him realize just how dangerous an error he'd made. He was giving her too much power, relinquishing too much of his control, laying it at her feet. It wasn't smart. They were coworkers. She blamed him for her brother's death. Guilt had a stranglehold on him, but his heart was desperate to break free and run wildly straight into her arms. He couldn't help himself.

Her hand came up between them. Her fingers rested on his lips. "Tell me about your father. Then you can kiss me."

A deep groan escaped Josh. "You drive a hard bargain." He didn't want to go there. Couldn't go there. But the promise of another kiss was alluring, tantalizing.

"And you think you're clever, but I know you too well, Josh."

His gaze on her mouth, he asked, "What does that mean?"

Her hand fell to her side and her lips twitched. "I know you think if you act all gooey I'll forget what I want to know. That's not going to happen."

Tenacious. Just like her brother. "I'm sorry to disappoint you, but I don't talk about my father. Ever."

The stubborn set to her jaw had him backing up. A sick feeling in the pit of his stomach made him shudder. She could easily find out the answers on her own. Maybe he should let her. Then he wouldn't have to see the pity, the revulsion on her face when she discovered the truth. "If you want to know so badly you can look it up. Have Linda do the research—that's what she's good at."

Serena caught his hand, her expression softening, beseeching him to confide in her. His heart sputtered, as longing to do just that swept through him like a tornado, wreaking havoc on his carefully constructed defenses. "I wouldn't invade your privacy like that. This is your story to tell. I'd rather hear it from you." She stepped closer, her sweet scent surrounding him, setting his senses on fire. "If you're going to let me in, Josh, then let me in."

He wanted to let her in so badly. He wanted to bury his face in her hair and spill his guts. But if he had an ounce of self-preservation, he wouldn't. Inhaling deeply through his nose, he slowly blew the air out in an effort to calm his racing heart. "My father died in prison."

Shock reverberated through Serena but she forced herself not to react. Keeping her expression as neutral as she could, she asked as gently as possible, "Prison? What was he in for?"

Josh swiped a hand over his face, looking suddenly tired and drawn. "Embezzlement."

She bit her lip. No wonder he hadn't wanted to tell her.

He leaned back against the opposite wall as if his legs couldn't support him anymore. "He'd been big into horse racing. Lost too much money betting on the wrong Thoroughbreds. To cover his debt, he stole from the customer accounts he managed in a small brokerage firm in town, depleted the life savings of so many people. He got caught."

Aching for Josh, Serena moved closer. "I'm so sorry. That had to have been devastating to you and your mom."

"It was."

The torment in his eyes seared her soul. Her breath caught.

"When he was convicted and sentenced, the whole town turned against us. My mother lost her job. The kids in school… It made living in Lamar unbearable," he said.

Anger on his behalf seeped into her tone. "That's not fair."

He let out a bitter-sounding laugh. "When is life ever fair? You of all people should know that."

His words dug deep into her own painful past. Her parents' fighting, their divorce, then Daniel's death. She'd had to dredge up every ounce of faith she had to not lose hope in God.

And instead she had laid the blame for Daniel's death on Josh.

Her heart beat wildly in her chest. An anxious flutter of something, some thought or emotion, tried to get her attention, but she pushed the need to forgive away. Josh was to blame. He should have been there for Daniel.

But that didn't lessen the anger and sympathy oozing through her on Josh and his mother's behalf. They'd suffered so much. He'd been so young. No wonder he kept people at a distance.

"You're right, life isn't fair." She laid a hand over Josh's heart. "God never promised fair, only that He'd see us through it."

Josh trapped her hand beneath his. His heartbeat pounded against her palm. "I was so angry. Angry at the world, angry at God."

"Yet you work in a soup kitchen run by a Christian church. Surely you haven't walked away from your faith."

"It took me a long time to make my way back to God. Helping those less fortunate made me realize that being angry over my circumstances was selfish. My dad paid the price for his bad behavior. We all paid the price. He broke my mother's heart. He broke everyone's heart."

Including Josh's. She hurt for him, hurt for what he'd

endured. "What led you to go into law enforcement?" she asked.

She waited, watching him work out his answer in his head. The play of light from the hall shadowed his strong jaw and deepened the contours of his cheekbones. He had a handsome face, not pretty, but masculine in the angles and planes. Her gaze dropped to his mouth, to the lips that had captured hers earlier in a playful kiss that had turned into something that left her breathless.

Tell me about your father. Then you can kiss me.

Her words echoed inside her head. Her pulse picked up speed. Would he take her up on the promise of a kiss? Did she want him to? A tumble of confusion assailed her. She did want him to, but she didn't, as well. If he did, would it mean something to him? It would to her and that scared her. Her heart was growing attached to this man.

"Not long after my dad's incarceration, I was in the local mini-mart. I didn't have any money but I wanted a candy bar so badly." He raised a hand and stared at his palm as if he were seeing the candy. "I stood there in the middle of the candy aisle with this chocolate bar in my hand, staring at it, thinking I could slip it into my pocket and no one would know. I knew stealing was wrong, my dad had just gone to prison for stealing, but the desire to take the candy was so strong, so hard to resist."

She ached for the boy he'd been. She couldn't imagine how hard the situation had been for him, losing his father and having the town ostracize him. She could picture him as a kid, all gangly legs and arms; her heart melted and affection blossomed. "Did you take the chocolate bar?"

"I didn't have the chance to make the decision before the owner caught me. He grabbed the bar out of my hand." His fingers curled before he dropped his hand to his side. "I can still hear Old Man Granger's voice in my head. 'I see the apple doesn't fall far from the tree.'"

"Oh, Josh." The hurt in his voice impaled her. The urge to hug him became unbearable. She slipped her arms around his waist and laid her cheek against his chest. His arms wrapped around her in a tight embrace. Beneath the fabric of the polo shirt he wore, his heart beat fast, the tempo matching the beating of her own rapid pulse.

"I ran," he said. "For three days, I lived in dread that the sheriff was going to come cart me away in handcuffs like he had my father."

Tears for the boy who'd lived in fear welled in her eyes. "But he didn't?"

"No. I turned myself in."

The deep rumble of his voice resonated through her. She pulled back to look at him. "What happened?"

"The sheriff was kind and took me seriously when he could have laughed me out of the building. When he asked my why I confessed to *almost* stealing, I told him I didn't want to be like my dad."

Serena swallowed back the lump in her throat. "You could never be like him."

"The sheriff said I could be anything I wanted." The tender look in his eyes caressed her face. "I wanted, want, to be the opposite of my dad."

"So you became a law enforcement officer," she said softly.

He nodded. His gaze rested on her lips. Yearning for the promised kiss tugged at her.

The world around them retreated, until there was nothing but them, this moment.

She leaned toward him, answering the question he'd not spoken.

Yes. She wanted him to kiss her again.

"What about you, Serena?" His gaze held her captive. "Why did you become a U.S. marshal?"

Grief pierced through the haze coating her mind.

She blinked, realizing how close she was to letting down her guard, to losing herself in the attraction and affection flaring between them. Slowly, she extracted herself from his embrace.

"Daniel." Her voice cracked. She wrapped her arms around her middle as if somehow she could hold in the grief as she held in the tears. "I followed Daniel into this career."

Sorrow crumpled Josh's expression. "I'm sorry."

His grief and remorse were unmistakable, laying siege to her heart. His hurt pierced her, forcing her to see him in a different way. He'd apologized numerous times. Until today her anger had never let her see that Josh, too, suffered. He did. Unshed tears burned her eyes. She knew she should forgive him. That was what God would want.

"I should have picked up the phone when he called. It wasn't until the next day that I listened to his message."

She shuddered with the force of her sorrow. "What did he say?"

Josh ran a hand through his dark hair. "I don't remember now. I could only bring myself to listen to it the one time."

Drawing the edges of her grief around her for protection, she asked, "Did you erase the message?"

He shook his head. "I couldn't bring myself to after the chief returned the phone to me."

Her heart thumped. "I'd like to hear it."

"Why? What good would it do?" The torment in his eyes was unmistakable. "I know you blame me. I blame myself. But listening to that message will only torture us both."

"Or it could provide a clue that will tell us what he was doing in that alley," she countered, her voice shaking with anger and dread. Hearing Daniel's voice would be torture, but she had to hear the message.

"If that's what you want."

"It is."

He closed his eyes as a spasm of pain marched across his face. Her heart ached for him. She didn't understand why she hurt for Josh. It was her brother who was dead. Because of Josh.

They both could have ended up dead.

Linda's words came back to Serena.

At one time she might have wished bodily harm to Josh. But now...

She had no idea how she felt about him, and the conflicted emotions were draining her dry.

When he opened his eyes, the flat hardness there stole her breath. He nodded and stepped back, creating a chasm that sent a shiver racing over her flesh.

"I'll get my other personal phone from my apartment for you tomorrow."

He walked away. It took every ounce of control she possessed not to chase after him.

Tomorrow would bring a better perspective. Tomorrow they could go back to how things were. Tomorrow the wall between them could go back up.

She'd make sure of it.

NINE

The morning sun streamed through the bedroom window. Serena groaned, grabbed a pillow and put it over her head to block out the brightness assaulting her eyes. She didn't want to face the day. Didn't want to have to go back to the role of Susan Andrews, and yet didn't want to go back to how things had been between her and Josh before this charade started.

How could she pretend to be in love with Josh when a part of her wasn't faking her feelings for him?

All night she'd wrestled with her conflicting emotions and finally realized that the crush she'd had on Josh long ago had blossomed instead of died, no matter how hard she'd tried to kill it. Not even the anger she harbored toward Josh for disregarding her brother's call could put an end to the attraction or stop the affection from spreading through her, filling all her empty places.

Hearing about his father, and seeing the anguish Josh carried because of what he and his mom went through, made him all too human. Glimpsing how good a couple they could be if they allowed themselves the luxury of a real relationship made her heart long for a reality where they could be together.

Utter nonsense.

This man was partly responsible for her brother's death.

That she had lessened her condemnation of Josh tightened her already strung-out nerves.

Forgiveness knocked at the door to her soul with an insistence that she couldn't ignore.

"Father in heaven, how do I forgive him?"

A verse of scripture whispered into her mind: *For if you forgive men their trespasses, your heavenly Father will also forgive you.*

Emotion clogged her throat. She'd heard that verse her whole life. She'd always considered herself a forgiving person.

Then why couldn't she forgive Josh?

Did that make her faith shallow? Was she only a fair-weather type of believer?

"Lord, I want to follow Your word, Your example. I need Your help."

She lay still for a long moment, hoping for a sign, some revelation that would show her how to let go of her anger.

When none materialized, she threw the pillow off her head and sat up. Taking deep, cleansing breaths, she told herself they had a job to do. A part to play. These roles they were playing were nothing more than a means to an end.

Emotion had no place in the equation. Yet her heart wouldn't release the soft feelings demanding attention so she could box them up and tuck them away.

She groaned.

For the past six months she'd resented being paired with Josh.

When she'd applied to be in the investigative operations division of the Marshals Service, she'd never expected she'd be tapped for a special operation like this one.

She'd wanted to delve into the tactical and strategic support side of apprehending fugitives, not tackle an investigation with a partner.

But that was before she realized how working closely with one person, relying on a partner, filled a void in her life she hadn't even realized was there.

She was so confused. Now she didn't know what she wanted.

However, she did know what she had to do. Finish the job of taking down the illegal adoption scam and bring the bad people to justice. Then find her brother's killer.

Tension knotted up her insides. Today she'd get to hear Daniel's voice again. Hear the message Daniel had left on Josh's phone. That had to be her focus. She had a feeling she'd need every ounce of courage to listen to the message.

All the personal stuff could be dealt with later.

With that thought firmly in place she readied herself for the day.

Twenty minutes later, dressed in another of the many Susan Andrews outfits she'd bought, Serena walked downstairs. The tantalizing scent of cinnamon and sugar teased her senses as she entered the kitchen. A tray of freshly baked cinnamon rolls sat on the counter. She found Josh sitting on a barstool drinking coffee and reading the paper. He was dressed in light-colored chinos and a patterned button-down with the sleeves rolled up. He looked younger, hip and oh, so appealing. She chewed the inside of her cheek.

Linda was humming an upbeat tune as she loaded the dishwasher.

With an effort Serena pulled her attention from Josh and helped herself to a roll and a cup of coffee. "You're spoiling us, you know that?" she said to Linda. "When we return to our own lives we're going to miss all the baked goods."

"Among other things," Josh muttered around a mouthful of cinnamon roll.

Serena jolted. "What?"

"The cars." His eyebrows rose. But the slight twitch of his mouth gave him away.

The teasing sent pleasure sliding through her. "O-kay."

She chose to take his statement at face value and ignore the undercurrent that suggested he would miss their charade for more personal reasons. It would be foolish to get caught up in what Josh thought and felt, especially when her whole being responded to him like a million particles of matter being drawn in by his magnetism.

"I'll have to admit this has been an enjoyable assignment so far," Linda said. "Baking, finding lost babies, watching you two fall in love."

Josh coughed into his cup.

Serena's face flamed. Linda had witnessed their kiss at the barbecue yesterday. That had to be the only reason she'd say something like that out of the blue.

"We're pretending." Serena glanced at Josh. His gaze met hers then bounced away. "What you saw yesterday was not real."

Linda grinned. "Sure looked real."

Josh set the paper down and stood, his movements as jerky as if he were struggling to recover from Linda's comments, too. "Colton Phillips called. They should arrive by noon." He glanced at the watch he'd bought for Jack. Jack, Josh had said, would wear a watch. "We better get going if we want to make it to church on time with the Johnsons."

Serena tucked in her chin. "I thought you were going to go to your apartment this morning." To get his phone.

He met her gaze. "We'll stop on the way back."

Disappointment settled in her chest. Serena would have to wait a little longer for Josh to retrieve his phone with Daniel's last message. Then finally she'd be able to find out what really happened in her brother's final moments. Could Josh have saved him?

"Linda, would you care to join us?" Serena asked, not only out of politeness but because she wanted—*needed*—a buffer between herself and Josh.

Taking off her apron, Linda said, "I'd love to."

After the church service, Josh drove to his apartment. Serena sat in the passenger seat; Linda in the backseat. They were all quiet. No one spoke. Josh figured the ladies were reflecting on the pastor's message about prayer being the link that kept people connected to God. He turned the concept over in his head. Though he prayed, he couldn't say he felt a link to God when he sent up requests for protection or for guidance. But then again, he didn't spend a lot of time in prayer or give much thought to trying to hear from God. Though he believed, even after the horrible way the town of Lamar had treated him and his mother, his faith remained nebulous. Serving in a soup kitchen during the holidays hardly qualified as commitment to God.

Maybe if he prayed more often or delved deeper into God's word, he'd feel more connected. More loved by God.

Something to ponder.

He parked at the curb outside the apartment building and climbed out of the sedan, saying, "I'll be right back."

Inside his apartment, he went straight to his desk in the corner of the living room. The cell phone was tucked away in the second drawer. Palming the device, he paused as a heaviness descended on his chest.

Bowing his head, he decided to do as the pastor suggested and prayed aloud, "Lord, forgive me. Forgive me for letting Daniel down. Letting Serena down. I pray, Lord, I'm not making a mistake by giving Serena this phone. I hope You'll protect her from being hurt worse by hearing Daniel's voice." Josh hesitated, unsure what else to say or ask. "Amen."

Shrugging, he left the apartment.

When he was back behind the wheel of the sedan, he offered Serena the phone.

She covered it with her hands as if he'd handed her a precious gift. "Thank you."

He wasn't sure she'd be thanking him after she heard Daniel's voice. But for now he'd take her gratitude.

They arrived back at the cover house and found U.S. marshal Colton Phillips, FBI agent Lisette Sutton and a young woman whom Josh guessed was Lonnie Bogler on the doorstep. The young woman couldn't be more than twenty. Her blond hair hung limply about her thin shoulders. The gauntness of her face emphasized the large size of her fear-filled eyes. There was no mistaking her fear. She was like a cornered rabbit, ready to bolt if given the chance.

Linda hustled everyone inside. Introductions were made as they moved into the living room. The way Colton touched the small of Lisette's back and how her gaze followed him weren't lost on Josh. The pair obviously had a thing going. One that was real, not pretend like he and Serena. They made an attractive couple, both blond and good-looking. Colton had come across as a maverick when he'd first come aboard, but Josh would count on him to have his back anytime.

Sensing that Lonnie would respond better to the women, Josh let Serena and Lisette take the lead. He hung back with Colton.

"How was she found?" Josh asked his fellow marshal in a low tone.

"An old news article in the Minneapolis paper on Baby Kay. After Kay disappeared, Lonnie left the city and went back home to Atwater. She saw the news piece last week and called the general information number in D.C. They routed her to Chief Harrison."

Josh winced. Lonnie's call would have been logged in

and would be easily accessible by anyone in the Marshals Service, which meant if the department leak were monitoring the logged calls, they'd know she'd been found. "Any trouble on your way here?"

Colton slanted him a glance. "There were a few times when I thought we were being followed. That's why it took us so long to get here. I doubled back a couple times just in case. As far as I can tell, we made it here undetected."

"Let's hope so."

"You're safe here," Lisette said to the frightened young woman. "Marshal Summers needs to hear your story."

Lonnie's breath audibly hitched. Her shoulders bowed as if she wanted to curl in on herself. "Is my baby safe?"

Sympathy for the younger woman's plight flooded Serena. She touched Lonnie's arm. Her skin felt clammy to the touch, which immediately concerned Serena. This girl had been in a bad way for a long time, but her skin bounced back, soft and pliant, not like that of someone who'd been using drugs for any amount of time. "We think so. Can you tell me what happened? Start from the beginning."

"Peter and me went to Minneapolis to get away from our families. They didn't approve of us." Lonnie winced. "We were so young and naive. Peter got a job for a freight company and I worked as a clerk in a drugstore. We had a small studio apartment." She gave them a weak smile. "I fixed it up real nice. But we were barely scraping by and we weren't getting along very well. Things weren't turning out like I'd dreamed they would." She sniffed, clearly fighting back tears. "When I found out I was pregnant, I thought things would change for the better."

Serena's heart ached for Lonnie.

Her breathing stumbled. "He wasn't happy about the baby, but we were making it work. After she was born…"

A fat tear crested Lonnie's lashes and dropped into her lap. "He left. He said he wasn't ready to be a daddy."

A stab of anger at Peter for not stepping up pierced Serena. Her gaze shot to Josh, wanting to see his reaction to Lonnie's tale. Josh stood near the doorway, his arms crossed over his chest, his face impassive. But she knew him well enough to realize the tic in his jaw meant he was as angered as she was.

"Go on, Lonnie." Lisette's voice brought Serena's mind back to Lonnie.

"I stayed in the apartment as long as I could before the landlord booted us. Little Kay and me lived in a shelter after that. One day this guy comes up to me and says he wants to buy my baby. I told him no. I loved my baby." The wildness in her eyes hurt Serena's heart. "I didn't want to give her up."

Patting her arm, Serena murmured, "I know, honey. You told the man no."

Lonnie dropped her gaze to her hands. "But he kept coming and pressuring me. He kept telling me I wasn't doing right by my baby. That there were people who couldn't have babies and they deserved one. I didn't." More tears spilled from her eyes. "He was right. I couldn't give her anything. Not even a bed of her own. But selling her to some random guy seemed wrong. I'm not stupid. I've heard stories of awful things people do to each other. I couldn't take the chance that this guy was a wacko who wanted to hurt my baby."

Seething for the young mother, Serena reined in her fury and remained quiet, letting the young woman get the story out.

"I decided I should take her somewhere safe. Give her to someone who'd take care of her. That's why I headed for the children's hospital. I thought they'd be able to help me find her a home."

"That's where you met Emma Bullock?" Serena asked.

Lonnie nodded. "I didn't know her last name. But yeah, she was super nice. I was sitting outside the hospital on a park bench and she had just come out of the hospital. She told me she was a nurse. She really liked Kay."

"Why did you leave Kay with her?" Josh questioned, his voice low, his tone intense.

Shooting a terrified glance his way, Lonnie said, "I'd left some of Emma's things at the shelter. I thought I should get them, but I didn't want to take Kay back there in case that guy showed up again. I thought if I left Kay with Emma then my baby would be safe." Her lip trembled. "We were supposed to meet up by a pub nearby. But when I returned, Emma and Kay were gone. I didn't know what to do. I was afraid I'd be arrested if I went to the police."

Refraining from telling Lonnie that she could have saved them all a lot of trouble had she come forward, Serena asked, "Can you describe the man who wanted to buy Kay?"

Lonnie nodded. "Dark and scruffy. Old. He had gray around here." She touched her temple. "And a scar across here." She gestured to her chin. "It was ugly. He was ugly and scary."

"Frank Adams," Josh stated. They'd already arrested Frank for assaulting Emma Bullock. He'd admitted to taking Baby Kay from her and giving the baby to some woman in a hotel. "Remember he said he'd given Kay to a woman. I'm almost positive it was Mrs. Munders."

"That seems the most likely possibility," Serena agreed.

"Who?" Lonnie asked. "Does she have my baby? Is she taking good care of her?"

"Mrs. Munders runs an adoption agency," Serena said. "We think someone paid Frank to grab your baby and hand her over to Mrs. Munders so she could put the baby up for adoption." Turning to Linda, Serena said, "Can you show her the picture?"

Linda hurried from the room and returned a moment later with the blown-up image taken from Mrs. Munders's collage of babies.

Lonnie stared at the photo and started sobbing. "That's her. Kay. My baby."

With that confirmation, Serena knew for sure Mrs. Munders had been involved in Kay's kidnapping. The evidence was falling into place. Now if they could only find the woman in the photo.

"What do we do with Lonnie now?" Colton asked.

Josh thought that was a fair question. They could charge the girl with child endangerment for not reporting the little one missing. A class A misdemeanor would net Lonnie up to a year in jail. But what good would that do. Lonnie was a scared kid herself. And she didn't know enough for her to be a real threat to Munders and his organization. But sending her away didn't feel right. At the moment Lonnie was resting in one of the guest rooms upstairs. Josh, Serena, Lisette and Colton sat around the dining table while Linda made lunch. She'd shooed them out of her domain when they'd offered to help.

"She can stay here with us," Serena said. "The house is certainly big enough. And we can protect her. We could say she's a niece come to visit."

"She isn't in any danger now," Josh countered. "She's told us what she knows, which isn't more than we already knew. Other than confirming Baby Kay's identity, there's no reason not to send her back to her home."

"But whoever hired Frank is still out there. They might think she knows more than she does," Serena argued and from the stubborn tilt to her chin he knew she wouldn't back down. "I think we should keep Lonnie in custody until we find the woman who has Baby Kay. Make sure the baby is well and happy. Let Lonnie have an opportunity to decide for herself if giving up her baby is truly what she wants to do."

"I agree," said Lisette, her green eyes serious. "She's young and made some mistakes, but she is the baby's mother. Though ultimately the courts will decide on custody."

Josh's gaze swung to Colton, who held up his hands. "Hey, not my call. I'm just the delivery man."

Turning his attention back to Serena, Josh opened his mouth to say no, but what came out was "We'll have to run it by the chief."

The smile on Serena's face melted the last of Josh's resistance. Oh, man. Last night he'd rationalized telling her about his father because he was acting in "Jack" mode. Now he had no excuse. Serena had peeled away all his protective layers and laid siege to his heart with her compassionate and caring nature. He would have to dig deep to find a crumb of defense. He was in so much trouble.

"I found her!" Linda's exclamation reverberated through the living room. She bustled in waving a sheet of paper.

"Who?" Serena set down the book she was reading. It was late in the evening. Colton and Lisette had long since left, returning to Colorado on an evening flight.

"The woman who has Kay." Linda set the paper onto the table. "Her name is Eve Cardinalli. She's forty-two and lives in Chesterfield. That's less than a half hour away."

Lonnie and Josh had been playing chess. Both looked up with stunned expressions.

Josh stood. "How did you find her?"

"The DMV database finally spit it out."

"Can we go see her?" Lonnie asked. The excitement in her voice tore at Serena.

Exchanging a concerned glance with Josh, Serena said, "Tomorrow. We'll go see her tomorrow."

Lonnie bit her lip. "What if she won't let me see Kay?"

Serena moved to sit beside Lonnie. "We'll cross that bridge when we get there. We don't know how she'll react."

Learning the adoption wasn't legal, that Baby Kay's birth mother hadn't had the chance to make the decision to give up her child, might send Eve running. They needed to know if this woman was aware of the illegal nature of the adoption, whom she'd dealt with and what information she could give them about the Perfect Family Adoption Agency.

Lonnie's chin quivered and tears gathered in her eyes. "I'm scared."

"There's no reason to be," Serena said. "We'll be with you."

"Do you think Kay is happy there with this woman?" Lonnie's eyes pleaded with Serena for reassurance.

"In the picture she looks happy" was all Serena could say.

Knowing how much money the adoption agency expected to be paid, Serena had no doubt Eve Cardinalli was providing well for Lonnie's child. But she refrained from saying so. Lonnie still had the right to take her child back.

After settling Lonnie in the guest room, Serena headed out to the back porch with Josh's cell phone in her hand. The day had gotten away from her, and she hadn't had a chance to listen to Daniel's message. In truth she wasn't as eager to push Play as she had thought she'd be. Josh had said it would be torture. Still, she had to know. She had to have this final closure. And she'd hear her beloved brother pleading for Josh to meet him or call him back. Hearing her brother's voice would be like ripping open a scabbed-over wound.

She sat on the back porch swing. Unlike last night, tonight the air was thick and oppressive with heat. Shadows played on the bushes butting up against the back fence. But her attention was on the phone. She powered it on. The muted LCD light glowed bright. Her finger hovered over the voice mail icon in the bottom left corner.

Movement in her peripheral vision sent her heart scattering and her pulse skittering. She pressed the phone against her thigh to cover the light as she slid off the swing into a crouch position and readied herself for an attack.

"Having second thoughts?"

Josh! She exhaled and rose. Her heart beat madly against her ribs. She peered into the darkness but couldn't see him; he stayed in the inky shadows of the yard. "You scared me. What are you doing out here?"

"Walking the perimeter. I do every night."

Keeping them safe. She smiled though she knew he couldn't see it. She resumed her seat and sent the swing swaying with the toe of her sandal.

Josh's silhouette, a darker stain against the pitch-black night, came slowly up the porch stairs. "Do you want to be alone?"

"Not really," she answered honestly.

He lowered himself to the seat beside her, stopping the motion of the swing. She held the phone on her lap, the light glowing eerily on Josh's face. Dredging up every ounce of courage she possessed, she pressed the icon that brought up the message screen. Her brother's name stared at her.

"Please, put it on speaker," Josh said softly.

With the tip of her finger she tapped the little arrow that would play the message and then the speaker icon.

Daniel's voice filled her head and settled in her heart.

"Hey, dude, get off your duff. Stop your wallowing. You should be working. A call came in and could be something big."

Serena's heart cracked into jagged pieces.

There was a strange noise for a few heartbeats; then, he said, *"Call me."*

Serena couldn't move. Couldn't breathe. Every fiber of her being longed for her brother. The anchor to her world. Without him she felt so lost. So alone.

Then Josh's arm slid around her shoulders, drawing her to his strong, muscled chest, anchoring her to the moment, to him. She wanted to cry the tears that had been choking her since the moment she heard of Daniel's murder. But they wouldn't come.

Josh had been right. It had been torture to hear Daniel's voice.

And frustrating because they were no closer to catching Daniel's killer.

TEN

Any second Josh would crumble beneath the crushing weight of guilt. Holding Serena in his arms, feeling her pain like a thousand tiny shards of glass, battered at his heart.

If only he'd answered his phone that day, Daniel wouldn't be dead. But he'd been so embroiled in his own problems with Lexi that he hadn't taken the call. And Daniel was dead.

Fighting to maintain his composure, Josh smoothed a hand down Serena's spine and cupped the back of her head with the other. "I'm so sorry. So sorry. It's my fault he's gone." The words would barely come, his throat constricted with anguish and remorse.

After a shuddering breath that vibrated against his shoulder, she lifted her head. "You were right." The bleakness in her voice tore at him.

"About?"

"That was awful." She slipped out of his arms. "I miss him so much."

"I do, too." Tears burned behind his eyelids. He held them back by sheer force of will. "I'll never forgive myself for not picking up the phone."

"Why didn't you answer?"

His mouth went dry. "I wanted to be left alone."

"Wallowing?"

He sank into the bench. "Lexi had broken up with me that morning."

She was silent for a moment. "I'm sorry. You must have loved her a great deal."

The strange note in her voice confused him. But her words scaled back a layer to his soul that revealed a truth he'd hidden. A truth that even now made him sweat. If he wasn't already seated, his legs wouldn't have held him upright.

He hadn't loved Lexi.

Not the way she wanted, needed, to be loved.

The sounds of the night filled the silence between them.

"We need to take this phone to the forensic team." She moved closer, and the scent of her wrapped around him, making him long to pull her back into his arms.

He tucked his hands under his thighs. "Why?"

"That noise," she said. "It sounded like he'd put his hand over the mouthpiece. People do that when they're interrupted. Someone talked to Daniel while he was leaving the message. Maybe the techs could enhance it enough to hear the voice. Maybe that person will know something to help us find my brother's killer."

He'd completely missed that. But Serena hadn't. Hope of finding a clue to Daniel's death pressed in on him, energizing him. He stood. "Tomorrow we'll take the phone to headquarters. Then we'll find Eve Cardinalli and find out what she knows. And hopefully reunite Lonnie with her baby."

His heart cramped to think of the heartbreak Eve Cardinalli would suffer when she learned the truth.

But the truth had to come out.

Serena rolled down the window of the new Suburban that had been delivered that morning as a replacement for the wrecked BMW. She needed some air because the tension inside the SUV was smothering.

They were on their way to Eve Cardinalli's house. Lonnie sat in the backseat next to Linda. Serena was glad Josh had agreed to bring Linda along, since Lonnie and Linda seemed to have bonded.

Josh sat at the wheel, silent, intense. There was an edginess to him that hadn't been there before. He had hardly spoken a word to Serena this morning when they'd met in the kitchen during breakfast. She'd pressed him to discuss a plan for meeting Eve Cardinalli, but he'd said little.

Because of Daniel.

She could guess that much.

Realizing why he'd taken a personal day and why he hadn't answered his phone had surprised her and made her feel terrible for him. He'd had his heart broken. Of course he'd needed time to process and deal with his emotions. How could she blame him for that? He had no way of knowing that by ignoring Daniel's call he was leaving his best friend alone to face a killer.

The need to forgive him bubbled within her chest. Daniel wouldn't want her to hold on to this antagonism and anger. Remorse for how she'd treated Josh throbbed beneath her breastbone.

"What if she won't let me see my baby?"

Lonnie's anxious voice broke through Serena's thoughts, forcing her to put her personal issues on hold. The job had to come first.

In the front passenger seat, Serena twisted around to look at the younger woman. Any way she looked at the situation, she knew someone was going to be hurt. "I know this is scary, Lonnie. But you'll have to trust us. We're going to make this right."

Linda patted Lonnie's hand. "Don't fret. Josh and Serena have a plan. They'll do what they need to in order to reunite you with your sweet baby girl."

Lonnie chewed her lip and nodded.

Serena faced forward to consult the directions to Ms. Cardinalli's house. "Take the next exit."

Once they hit Chesterfield, it wasn't hard to find the address. As they rolled through Eve's neighborhood, Serena couldn't help but think the upscale houses ranging from medium to large on lots with well-cared-for lawns seemed like an idyllic place to raise a family. Children played in the yards. Dogs barked from porches. Parents suspiciously eyed the big black vehicle invading their community. She couldn't fault their caution.

Josh pulled the SUV to the curb in front of Eve's house, a cute two-story home set back from the road. A white picket fence enclosed a yard of lush green grass. A tree near the edge of the house provided shade for a golden retriever.

As Serena climbed out, the dog pushed to his feet, his tail raised.

Josh came around the front end of the car and joined Serena on the sidewalk. "Nice place."

"It is." Serena glanced back at the vehicle. Lonnie's nose was pressed against the window, her large eyes taking in the house, the yard and the dog.

"Let's get this over with." Josh started up the walkway along the edge of the white fence.

Serena fell into step with him. The dog let out a bark and loped toward the fence.

"Hey, boy," Josh said, holding out his hand, palm facing down. "It's okay. We're the good guys."

"How do you know it's a boy?" Serena asked.

"Just guessing."

The dog sniffed Josh's hand then licked him before turning his attention to Serena.

She shook her head, tucking her hands behind her back. "No way am I letting you lick me, dog."

Josh's amused chuckle warmed her cheeks.

The front door opened. A woman with dark hair pulled back into a loose ponytail and dressed in shorts and T-shirt stood in the doorway. Her green eyes regarded them warily. Her gaze darted to the SUV at the curb and bounced back. "Can I help you?"

"Are you Eve Cardinalli?" Josh asked, his voice losing all trace of humor.

"Yes. And you are?"

Josh showed her his badge. "Deputy U.S. Marshals Josh McCall and Serena Summers."

Eve peered at the gold star then lifted her worried gaze to meet Serena's. "What can I do for you?"

"Can we come in?" Serena asked with a gentle smile. The woman was skittish. Did she know that she'd illegally adopted her daughter?

"What is this about? Does this have something to do with Tim?" Her eyes hardened. "We're divorced and have been for over a year. If he's in some kind of trouble, I don't want to know. I haven't seen him in months."

"This has nothing to do with your ex-husband," Josh stated. "Did you recently adopt a baby girl from Perfect Family Adoption Agency?"

Eve tucked in her chin. The worry returned to her eyes. "Yes." She looked at Serena. "Is there a problem?"

Serena shared a glance with Josh before answering. "Yes, Eve, there is."

Placing a hand on her middle as if to quell a bout of sudden nerves, Eve stepped back, allowing them to enter the house. The inside of the home was as quaint as the outside. Cherrywood floors stretched down a hall leading to a kitchen.

Eve led them to the living room. Toys littered the sea of blue carpet.

Gesturing to the brown leather couch, Eve said, "Please, have a seat."

Serena sank onto the soft cushion. Josh folded himself next to her, their knees touching. A week ago—a day ago, actually—she would have scooted away, creating some distance, but she remained in place, comforted by the feel of him next to her.

Eve sat across from them on a matching love seat. A coffee table separated them.

"Eve, what can you tell us about Perfect Family Adoption?" Josh asked.

She shrugged. "They were wonderful to me. Matilda Munders was like a fairy godmother. She found little Crystal for me. I owe her my happiness."

"Do you know where the baby came from?" Serena asked.

Eve shook her head. "Not really. I mean, I didn't meet the birth mother, if that's what you're asking. It was a closed adoption." Her eyes widened. "Is there something wrong with the birth mother? Is Crystal ill? In danger?"

Serena held up her hand. "No, nothing like that."

Josh leaned forward, drawing Eve's attention. "The problem is that the baby, your Crystal, was kidnapped from her birth mother."

"What?" Eve covered her mouth with her hand. Lowering her voice, she said, "That can't be true. Mrs. Munders said the birth mother was a young girl who didn't want her baby."

"It's true Lonnie, the birth mother, is young. But she hadn't made the decision to give up her daughter," Serena explained. "A man whom we believe was working for Perfect Family used intimidation and scare tactics to try to coerce Lonnie into giving up Baby Kay. When that didn't work, he kidnapped Kay."

Eve shook her head. "You're wrong. Mrs. Munders wouldn't have done that. She's a good Christian woman." Tears filled Eve's eyes. "Please, there has to be a mistake."

From the woman's reaction, Serena was certain she hadn't known that her daughter had been illegally put up for adoption. "Does Crystal have a square strawberry mark on her cheek?" Serena asked gently.

Slowly, Eve nodded. "I think I'm going to be sick." She leaned forward, putting her head between her knees.

Serena moved to sit next to her and rubbed her back. "I know this is a shock. We really need to know everything you can tell us about your dealings with Perfect Family."

"I'll tell you anything—just don't take my baby away from me," came Eve's muffled reply.

Serena met Josh's gaze. He arched an eyebrow. They both knew they couldn't make such a promise.

Heaving a sigh, Serena decided to be forthright with Eve. "Look, we can't guarantee you anything at this point. Lonnie, Baby Kay, uh, Crystal's birth mother, is outside in the car."

Eve straightened. Tears stained her cheeks. Her lips trembled. "She wants her baby back, doesn't she?"

"I don't know what Lonnie wants," Serena said. "I don't want to give you false hope. Lonnie would like to see her baby."

"Crystal's napping. She usually wakes about eleven."

Josh checked his watch. "That's in a half hour. Time enough for you to tell us about the adoption agency."

Eve tucked her hands beneath her arms as if she were holding herself together. "Tim and I couldn't have children. We tried everything. When it became apparent there was a problem with me, Tim—" She pressed her lips tight as a spasm of pain crossed her face. "He wanted children.

His own children. He left me. Found someone who could give him what he wanted. He didn't even wait for the divorce to be final."

Serena's jaw clenched. What was it with these men? First Lonnie's Peter ditched her because she *had* a baby and then Eve's Tim ditched her because she *couldn't have* a baby. Sometimes humans were really disappointing. Serena wondered how God felt when His creations acted so selfishly.

Her own selfish behavior toward Josh reared with stunning force.

But she couldn't deal with that right now. She had to stay focused on the job. Be professional.

"So you decided to adopt on your own," Josh prompted.

Eve nodded but kept her gaze on Serena. "It cost me all my savings and part of the money Tim paid me from his investments. Investments I knew nothing about, I might add."

"Why did you choose Perfect Family to adopt through?" Serena asked.

"I was a clerk at the courthouse in downtown St. Louis. I was telling a coworker that I was thinking of adopting. She said she'd heard one of the judges saying that Perfect Family Adoption was the place to go. So I made an appointment. Matilda was so nice." She made a face. "I guess she had me fooled."

"She does come across as nice," Serena agreed.

"Do you remember the name of the judge?" Josh asked.

Eve glanced in his direction and shook her head. "No. But I'm sure if you asked Shirley she'd be able to tell you. I should have done my due diligence and checked the agency out. Especially when Matilda had a baby for me so quickly." She stared at Serena. "I didn't know."

Josh sat forward. "Do you have the adoption papers?"

"I do."

Serena liked where Josh was going with this. "Can we see them?"

Even though Dylan McIntyre most likely had generated the documents, the papers would be on Munders's letterhead. Not enough to indict Fred Munders, but at least enough to implicate him and his partners in the law firm.

Eve left the room and came back a few moments later with a thick envelope in hand. She sat back down before offering Serena the package. "Here's everything pertaining to Crystal's adoption."

Taking the documents, Serena said, "Thank you. This will help a lot."

The faint cry of a baby alerted them that little Crystal was awake.

Eve jumped to her feet. "I'll need to change her diaper then I'll bring her down." Squaring her shoulders, she added, "Please invite Lonnie in."

Admiring Eve for the brave way she was handling the situation, Serena rose and took her hand. "Thank you."

A tear slipped down Eve's cheek. "It'll break my heart to give her up."

Josh stood. "Serena, go with Eve," he said, his voice low, intent. "I'll get Lonnie."

Serena stared at him for a second. He thought Eve might try to run with the baby. Accepting his caution, she nodded and followed Eve upstairs. Eve led her to the last room. The door was decorated with flowers and a decal spelling out *Crystal*.

The room was a princess's dream. Soft pink walls, a mural depicting a forest with animated animals frolicking about on a hill with a castle at the top.

An expensive-looking wooden crib dominated one corner of the room. Lying in the middle of the crib, feet up in the air and hands waving, nine-month-old Baby Kay gurgled happily.

Eve picked her up and hugged her tight. "Hey, sweet girl. How's my baby?"

Serena's heart pounded as tenderness flooded her system, stirring up a longing she'd been ignoring. At twenty-seven she hadn't thought she was ready for motherhood, but she couldn't deny how much the idea appealed to her now. Must have been the whole charade of wanting to adopt a baby that had these urges roaring to life.

After Eve changed the baby's diaper and put a fresh outfit on her, they went downstairs where Josh, Linda and Lonnie waited in the living room.

Lonnie gasped as they entered the room. "She's gotten so big."

Serena's heart lurched as Eve went directly to the younger woman. "I'm Eve."

Lonnie's gave her a shy smile but made no move to take the baby from Eve's arms. "I'm Lonnie, Kay's—" She swallowed. "I named her Kay after my grandma."

Tears streamed down Eve's face. "Kay's a pretty name. I named her Crystal."

Wiping at the tears filling her eyes, Lonnie sniffed. "That's pretty, too."

Linda slipped an arm around Lonnie. "Why don't we all sit down and get to know one another?"

Serena sent Linda a grateful smile. The older woman knew how to take charge of the strained situation. The two women were in good hands.

Lonnie and Eve, holding the little brown-eyed, brown-haired baby, sat on the couch.

Josh cupped Serena's elbow and gestured with his head for her to follow him outside. With one last look at the women and the baby, Serena followed.

"I'll guarantee the judge was Simon Simms," Josh said.

She nodded. "Dylan McIntyre said the judge signed off on all the adoption paperwork. But we don't know if he's culpable or was duped into believing the Munderses were on the up-and-up."

"True. We need that meeting with Fred Munders," Josh stated. "I'm calling him."

Serena gripped the thick envelope with a mix of apprehension and anticipation.

Josh took out his cell phone and dialed. When he was connected to Fred Munders, he put the call on speakerphone.

A deep, gravelly voice came on the line. "This is Fred Munders. What can I do for you, Mr. Andrews?"

"We've been in the process of adopting through your wife's agency," Josh stated. "But I've yet to see the contract."

"I will make sure Matilda has it in hand shortly."

Josh frowned. "I'd rather deal with you on this."

"The agency is my wife's company, Mr. Andrews. Everything goes through her."

Serena rolled her eyes. Somehow she doubted that old Fred didn't have his hands on the reins of the agency. Matilda might be good at dealing with prospective parents, but Serena doubted she had the mental faculties to run the business end, as well.

"I heard you're the one I need to speak with. That you'd be able to get my wife a baby on the fast track."

Serena worried that Josh was pushing too hard.

"Really? Now where would you have heard something like that?"

"Judge Simms mentioned it."

Mouth gaping, Serena shook her head, certain that would send up a red flag to the lawyer.

"He was mistaken," Fred finally said.

"I'm willing to pay a finder's fee," Josh stated. "Top dollar. In the seven-figure range if you can put a child in my wife's arms by the end of the month."

Serena pinched the bridge of her nose. He'd blown it for sure now.

There was a moment of silence. "A sizable deposit is required for all transactions."

Josh's triumphant grin had Serena shaking her head.

"That won't be a problem," Josh said. "Can I bring the money to your office?"

"No. We'll meet at the Park Avenue Coffee Shop near Lafayette Square. Tomorrow at ten in the morning."

Giving Serena a thumbs-up, Josh gushed, "Wonderful. Will you take a cashier's check?"

"That would be acceptable. Have it made out to Perfect Family Adoption Agency."

"I can do that," Josh said with a smug smile. "Until then, Mr. Munders."

The line clicked off.

A bad feeling settled in the pit of Serena's stomach. "Josh, I don't know about this. What if you're being set up?"

What if she lost him, too? Her heart contracted painfully in her chest. She couldn't stand the thought of him getting hurt. Or worse.

"It will be fine," Josh assured her as he tucked his phone back into his pocket.

"But you don't know that." Serena fisted her hands. "I'm sure Daniel thought whatever he was doing would turn out all right, too. And it didn't."

Hurt flashed in Josh's eyes. "I'll have you as backup."

"Too many dead bodies have been turning up connected to this case," she insisted. "Fred's expecting you alone. What if I can't get to you in time? What if something awful happens to you?"

He cupped her cheek. "Serena, what is this? You can't let your nerves get the better of you now."

"It's not nerves. It's caution."

But she knew the riot going on inside of her was more than paranoia. Call it the feeling of dread, intuition, a hunch or just plain old fear; she had a strong sense that something horrible was going to happen when Josh met with Fred Munders.

She would have to make sure she was there to guard him with her life, because she couldn't lose him. Not like she'd lost Daniel.

She was certain she wouldn't survive that.

ELEVEN

Josh followed Serena back inside Eve Cardinalli's home. He wasn't sure what to make of Serena's upset. She'd seemed genuinely worried about his well-being. After last night, he was so confused about Serena and her feelings for him. He didn't know whether to be annoyed, worried or encouraged.

The fact Serena was concerned for his welfare certainly marked a turning point in their relationship. Could she care for him? Hope built inside his heart, but he pushed it away. He couldn't let emotions distract either of them from their goal—to get the evidence they needed to bring down the Munderses and break up the illegal adoption ring.

But it was hard to stay on task with Daniel's murder hanging around his neck like an albatross, reminding him constantly of his failure. Looking at Serena, being with her, only added weight to his guilt. And last night had tightened the noose, making each breath he took harder and harder, until there were times he thought he'd welcome oblivion.

Especially when she'd insisted on listening to her brother's message.

As he'd predicted, it had been painful for her to hear Daniel's voice.

Seething rage clouded his vision for a moment, blocking out the women in the living room. Whoever killed Daniel would pay dearly. He'd see to it. For Daniel, for himself and most especially for Serena.

If only they knew what Daniel had been working on.

His gaze went to Serena. Admiration flooded him. She was such a smart woman. He'd completely missed that Daniel had interrupted the message he'd been leaving to talk with someone else. But Serena had caught it. Her idea to take the phone to forensics was brilliant. They'd dropped the phone off at the St. Louis crime lab on their way out of downtown. The techs had promised to work on it as soon as possible and report directly to them.

Tuning in to the women's conversation, Josh heard Eve say, "We've been talking, making some plans." She smiled at Lonnie and handed her the child. "We decided that Crystal's full name will be Crystal Kay."

"That's lovely," Serena said.

"Eve has invited me to stay here with her and Crystal Kay," Lonnie said, her big eyes alight with joy as she bounced the little girl on her hip.

Serena's slight wince matched the trepidation marching through Josh. He wasn't sure that was a good idea. He was afraid both of the women would get hurt. He met Linda's gaze and raised an eyebrow in question.

"I know what you're both thinking," Linda said. "But Eve and Lonnie both understand that custody of Crystal will need to be determined by the courts. But this way they can get to know each other."

Serena turned to Lonnie. "And you're okay with this?"

"Yes." Lonnie nodded her head emphatically. "I can't take Crystal Kay from Eve. I can tell how much they love each other." Her big eyes filled with tears. "Besides, what can I offer her? Certainly not a life like this."

Tucking an arm around Lonnie's shoulders, Eve said, "I want to give both of them a home. Lonnie's home life isn't good." Smiling despite the tears running down her face, she said, "And I don't want to be alone. If I can have two daughters to care for, that would be wonderful." Eve tucked a curl behind Crystal's ear. The child turned toward her and held out her chubby arms. Lonnie easily relinquished her hold, and Crystal went into Eve's embrace.

Serena hugged Lonnie. "You know there's someone else who'd like to know that Baby Kay, Crystal Kay, has been found and is safe."

"Emma," Lonnie said.

"Yes. We'll call the Minneapolis police and let Detective Jones know. He'll contact Emma."

"Thank you. I'd like to see Emma and thank her for trying to protect Crystal Kay."

"We can pass on Eve's phone number," Josh interjected. "If that's all right with you, Eve?"

"Yes, please," Eve said, her tears drying. "Lonnie told me what happened. It's just appalling."

"Yes, it is. But we're doing everything we can to put a stop to the criminals."

They were close. Josh could feel it. Tomorrow's meeting with Fred Munders would produce results. Results that would put Fred Munders and everyone else connected to the illegal adoption ring behind bars.

Later that night, Serena couldn't sleep. She tossed and turned, her mind a jumble of worry over what would happen tomorrow when Josh met with Fred Munders. The lawyer was smart. He hadn't said anything that could be construed as illegal, and he was having Josh meet him away from his office.

At least in the coffee shop nothing bad could happen to Josh. Too many witnesses. But then again, a sniper's bullet could easily find its mark.

She was being ridiculous. There was no reason to think

Munders suspected Jack Andrews was anything other than what he appeared to be. They'd covered all their bases. There was an office downtown with Jack's name on it. The fact that Josh was hardly there didn't matter. The receptionist for the bank had forwarded the one call that had come in from the adoption agency to Josh's cell phone.

There was no reason to be so twisted up inside. Josh would be fine. He would get Munders to incriminate himself and then they could move in to arrest him.

Her mind then jumped to the cell phone. The forensics team hadn't called yet. It could be days before the techs had time to work on the voice message. She sent up a prayer that they would be able to isolate another voice so they could hear who Daniel was talking to. And hopefully, identify him or her. That person had a lot to answer for.

Finally giving up on sleep, she decided to go downstairs to retrieve the book she'd been reading, which she'd left on the coffee table in the living room. The thriller would at least keep her mind occupied until she grew drowsy enough to rest.

After donning a pair of slippers, she made her way down the dimly lit hall past Josh's room. There was no light beneath his door. She envied him the ability to fall asleep.

Downstairs she went, first to the kitchen for a glass of water and then into the living room. The second she stepped into the room, she froze. Awareness prickled her skin. She wasn't alone.

Her gaze searched the dark room. Was that a person sitting by the window?

She groped for the light switch. Found it and flipped it up. The overhead light flared bright, revealing Josh. He'd pulled one of the armchairs to the window. He blinked at her owlishly. He had on basketball shorts and a T-shirt, making him look young and carefree. His feet were bare and his hair mussed in a cute way that had her pulse jumping.

After her heart left her throat so she could speak, she asked softly, "Couldn't sleep, either?" She stood rooted to the spot, feeling self-conscious in her oversize tee and silk capri pants.

Fortunately, he didn't seem impressed. He turned back to the window. "I thought I heard something."

Caution tripped down her spine. She flipped the light off. Using the excuse of picking up her book lying on the side table, she moved to stand beside him and stared out the front window. All appeared peaceful in the neighborhood. The houses dark with people tucked safely in for the night. "Anything out there?"

"Not that I can detect. I walked the perimeter twice and secured all the locks on the doors and windows."

There was an undertone of attentiveness in his voice that tightened her chest. "But you still feel uneasy."

Now that her eyes had adjusted to the shadows again, she watched him scrub the back of his neck with his hand.

"Yes. There's no reason for it," Josh said, his voice low. "We're safe. I'm probably keyed up about tomorrow."

Tucking her book under the arm that held her glass of water, she laid her free hand on his shoulder. "Don't discount your gut feeling. Sometimes that's how God talks to us."

He covered her hand with his, the pressure warm and thrilling. "Thanks. I'll remember that. I talked to the chief. He and Agent Bishop looked at the adoption papers Eve gave us. Fred Munders's signature is on them."

A spurt of triumph had Serena squeezing his shoulder. "That's terrific. Then you don't need to meet with Munders tomorrow. Between Fred's signature on the paperwork and testimony from Dylan and Eve, the attorney general should have no problem indicting Fred and Matilda Munders."

"I asked the chief to tell the AG to hold off doing anything until after my meeting with Fred tomorrow. If I can get him to say something incriminating, then the case would be a slam dunk."

A ripple of anxiety skittered over her. "But why take the unnecessary risk?"

"Because I want to do it right. Make the case airtight." Linking his fingers through hers, he stood, signaling an end to the discussion. "I suggest we both go to bed and get some sleep."

Her stomach tied up in knots, Serena allowed him to lead her upstairs. Josh walked her to the door of her room. He released her hand. "Good night, Serena."

"Josh," she said, stopping him before he could walk away. The dimly lit hallway threw shadows over Josh's face, hiding his eyes. The words bubbled up and spilled out. "I don't blame you for Daniel's murder. Do I wish you'd picked up the phone that day? Yes, of course. But I was wrong to put the fault on you. You couldn't have known what would happen." She wished she could make him see the truth that had taken her so long to see. "You need to give yourself a break."

"That will never happen."

The hardness of his voice hurt her heart. "At some point you'll have to forgive yourself. Or you'll always be burdened by unnecessary guilt. You can regret not picking up the phone, but you don't get to feel guilty for his death."

He reached past her to open her door. "Go to bed, Serena. We have a big day tomorrow."

Then he was striding down the hall and disappearing into his own room. With a sigh, she stepped inside and closed the door. Once settled back in bed with the bedside lamp on and her book open, she couldn't focus on the words on the page.

She hurt for Josh. She winced thinking of all the ways in which she'd been mean to him, unjustly condemning him for Daniel's death. And he'd taken her punishment without a word.

Setting the book aside, she turned off the light and lay back, praying for Josh until sleep claimed her.

A crash jolted Serena awake. Her heart pounded in large beats as the echo of the noise reverberated through her head. She threw aside the covers, grabbed her gun from the holster hanging on the nearby chair and raced out of the room.

She met Josh in the hall. Light spilled from his room, illuminating the tension on his face. He held his weapon at his side.

"You okay?" he whispered.

"Yes." She glanced toward the stairs descending into darkness. "The noise came from downstairs."

They hurried to the lower floor. The entryway light came on, and Linda met them at the bottom of the stairs. Belting her blue terry robe tighter, she said, "I heard a window breaking. Sounded like it came from the den."

"You two go upstairs. I've got this," Josh whispered in an urgent tone.

She drew back as indignation flooded her. "Excuse me? I've got your back."

Linda reached her hand inside the pocket of her robe to withdraw her weapon. "And I've got *your* back."

Josh pressed his lips together. "Fine." Holding his weapon in a two-handed grip, he moved quietly toward the closed den door. He reached for the door as the lights in the house winked out, throwing the world into a pitch-black void.

Serena's heart pounded in her throat. The darkness disoriented her. She pressed her back against the wall and reached with her free hand to grab a handful of Josh's T-shirt.

Another loud crash sounded. This time it came from the kitchen. Serena jerked, her nerves jumping.

Linda touched Serena's shoulder. "Do either of you have a phone on you?"

Wincing, Serena shook her head. Then realizing neither could see her, she whispered back, "It's on my bedside table."

"Mine, too," Linda said. "Josh?"

"Upstairs. You two go up. Use Serena's phone to call for backup."

Serena tightened her hold on his shirt, with the need to defend him, protect him, filling her. "I'm not leaving you."

"I'll go up," Linda stated. "You two don't get yourselves killed."

Serena sensed Linda move away. Serena sent up a prayer of protection for Linda and her and Josh. "Den or kitchen?"

"Den. On three we go in. You peel right and stay low. I'll go left."

Swallowing back the trepidation closing off her breathing, Serena sought calm. She'd trained for situations like this. But the reality was tough, harder on the senses because the stakes were so high. A wrong move, and one or both of them could end up dead.

"One."

She released her hold on Josh.

"Two."

Steeling her nerves, she prepared herself to breach the den.

The scuff of a shoe behind her sent her senses on alert. She whipped around, aiming her gun into the oppressive blackness. Someone was there, inching their way toward them. Her mind scrambled with possibilities. The person could be wearing night-vision goggles. They were easy targets. She needed to protect her partner.

Josh's hand, on her shoulder, tugged her toward the front door. Stepping backward, she moved with Josh past the closed den door on her left.

Gunfire exploded, the barrage assaulting her senses and hurting her ears.

Josh shouted, shoving her to her defensive squat position. "Down!"

Muzzle flash put the shooter at the end of the staircase. Her pulse tripped. The guy was close. Too close.

Bullets slammed into the front door.

More hit the walls.

Thud, thud, thud.

The sound echoed inside Serena's head.

Josh fired over her right shoulder. She aimed for the spot where she'd seen the flash of light from the attacker's gun.

The den door opened. The faint glow of the moon illuminated the hallway.

A second man's silhouette filled the door frame; he held a large-caliber weapon.

Surprise jolted Serena.

He aimed in their direction.

Serena aimed at the man in the doorway and pulled the trigger. He staggered back with a yelp of agony.

The other assailant fled, the sounds of his feet pounding on the wood floor barely discernible over the echo of noise battering at Serena's eardrums, making her head pulse with pain.

Josh sprinted after the intruder. "Stop!"

The retort of a single gunshot was muffled by the ringing in Serena's ears. The assailant screamed and crumpled to the ground.

The silence pressed in on Serena. Was Josh safe? Linda? She lurched to her feet.

Then Josh was at her side, his strong hands on her shoulders.

"Are you hit?" His hands moved restlessly down her arms and back up to cup her face.

She shook her head then searched him for signs of injury. "You?"

"No."

Relieved, she melted against him. His heart thudded against her cheek. A welcome sound that drowned out the echo of gunfire.

The attack had lasted only a minute or two, but Serena felt as if the siege had taken a year off her life.

Sirens drew close.

"Josh! Serena!" Linda's concerned cry broke them apart. She ran down the stairs and skidded to a halt on the hardwood floor.

"Here," Josh called out. "By the front door. We're okay. You?"

"Good. Sounds like the cavalry is here."

Josh tugged Serena to her feet, opened the front door and stepped out onto the front porch. Red-and-blue lights flashed as several police cruisers screeched to a halt at the curb. Uniformed officers ran from their cars.

Releasing Serena, Josh stated his identity and took control of the situation, leading the officers into the house. Admiring Josh's calm, she tried to steady herself. Adrenaline still pumped edgy energy through her veins.

Not about to miss out on the action, Serena followed them back inside. Flashlights illuminated a man lying on the den rug, clutching his thigh where her bullet had torn a hole through his flesh. A dark crimson stain spilled onto the floor, pooling around him.

She crouched next to him and recited the Miranda before asking, "Who sent you? Who do you work for?"

"I need a doctor," the man groaned.

"The lady asked you a question." Josh stood next to Serena, his hand resting lightly on her shoulder.

"I want a lawyer!"

Serena blew out a frustrated breath. Protocol dictated she couldn't question him now that he had asked for legal representation. Her fingers curled.

"Paramedics are here," an officer said from the doorway of the den.

"Come on," Josh said, squeezing her shoulder. "Let's give them some room."

They moved out of the way so a pair of EMTs could tend to the suspect's wound.

"Keep an officer with him," Josh said to the nearest policeman. "We've had too many people working for the organization end up dead before we could get any information out of them."

Linda appeared in the doorway and motioned to them.

Stepping into the entryway, Josh said, "What about the guy I shot in the kitchen?"

"He'll live," Linda said with a dose of anger in her voice. "A shoulder wound. But he's not talking. Asked for his lawyer."

"So did this one," Serena said, gesturing toward the den. "How do you think they found us?"

Josh ran a hand down his face. "Either the leak in the office found out where we are or they were watching Eve Cardinalli's house and followed us back."

Alarm sucked the breath from Serena's lungs. "Eve and Lonnie could be in danger!"

Josh whirled around and ran outside. Serena and Linda hurried after him.

Josh grabbed the nearest patrolman. "You need to get a unit out to Chesterfield. We have witnesses that need protection."

"Yes, sir." The officer took the address and called for a cruiser to go to Eve's house.

Linda dialed Eve's number. "I'm going to let Eve and Lonnie know what's going on. They need to take precautions."

Serena poked Josh's arm. "Our cover's been blown."

"Not necessarily. If we can keep these two thugs from talking to anyone until after the meeting with Fred Munders tomorrow, we should be good."

Apprehension tightened the muscles in Serena's shoulders. She didn't like *ifs*. *Ifs* were unpredictable. Tomorrow could be a trap, and Josh would be the one caught in the snare. She fought back a wave of panic.

"Jack? Susan?"

Trina and Darrell rushed over. Serena hid her gun behind her leg. Josh tucked his behind his back, slipping it into the waistband of his shorts. All along the street, neighbors stood on their porches, watching the chaotic scene unfolding at the new neighbor's house. Serena could only imagine how fearful they must be, thinking that their once safe and peaceful neighborhood had been touched by danger.

"Is everything okay?" A clump of Darrell's hair was standing straight up. "We heard gunshots."

"I was so scared. And so thankful the boys are away at a sleepover." Trina seized Serena's hand. "You must have been terrified!"

"I was," Serena answered, realizing the truth in the words. No amount of training could prepare anyone for a real-life situation like they'd just experienced. Being trapped and cornered was an officer's worst nightmare. Her worst nightmare come to life. She shuddered.

The paramedics wheeled out one of the assailants.

"Oh, my." Trina held a hand to her throat. "Who shot him?"

"I did," Josh said. "I've got a concealed handgun license. Up in Alaska, everyone carries."

Bless Josh for his quick reply. Serena smiled at her "husband." "Jack's my hero."

Trina turned to her husband. "Maybe you should get a gun. This neighborhood isn't as safe as we thought."

"I'm sure this is an anomaly," Linda said, joining them on the sidewalk. "Susan, Jack, the police would like a word."

"Of course." Serena smiled reassuringly at Trina. "It's all over now. You two head on home. Get some sleep before the alarm goes off. We're good."

The couple left but didn't head to their house. Instead, they crossed the street to talk to the other neighbors. Serena hoped none of them noticed she was holding a gun. As she hurried up the front steps she pressed the weapon against her belly. The lights were back on in the house. Linda ushered them into the den and shut the door.

"I just talked to the chief. He isn't happy to hear about the break-in. He wants to pull the plug on this operation. The AG is chomping at the bit to indict Fred and Matilda Munders. The chief stalled him until noon."

"Perfect," Josh said with grim satisfaction. "That's plenty of time for my meeting with Munders."

Serena's chest tightened. Her gaze sought Josh's. Tomorrow their undercover marriage would come to an end, one way or another.

With a shock, she realized she didn't want it to end.

She'd fallen in love with Josh. And she had no idea what to do about it.

TWELVE

"He's late," Josh groused into his coffee cup, knowing the small microphone hidden in the button of his shirt would pick up his words despite the ambient noise of the coffee shop. Behind the counter, the hiss of steaming milk from the espresso machine competed with the low levels of conversation from the half dozen patrons and the overhead speakers pumping out soft classical music.

"Patience is a virtue," Serena's soft and lyrical voice hummed into his ear through the earpiece he'd inserted before entering the Park Avenue Coffee Shop.

He was tempted to look over to where she sat in the corner booth by the barista station and make a face at her. But that would give away her position and put both of them in danger. He hated that she was here in the first place. Oh, he wanted the backup, but the thought of anything happening to her made his blood run cold. She might not be his "wife" but she was more than his partner. Their kisses hadn't been fake. Nor were the feelings swelling in his heart.

He glanced through the window to his left and watched the traffic drive by, the pedestrians going about their morning, and he kept an alert eye out for the suspect who they believed was the mastermind behind the illegal baby-adoption ring. "That particular virtue is overrated, as you well know."

Serena's light chuckle tickled his ear. "Come on, Josh. It took us ten minutes longer than it should have to get here. Traffic's a bear this morning."

True. Road construction had delayed their arrival. "I'll give him another fifteen minutes."

"Then what? You gonna storm the castle?"

He smiled slightly at her attempt at levity. "Yeah, actually, that's exactly what I plan to do. Raid Munders's law firm and arrest him."

"I wish you'd move farther inside, away from the window," Serena said, concern evident in her tone. "You're too exposed there."

They'd had this argument when they arrived. She'd wanted him to take one of the back corner tables. He'd wanted to sit outside. She'd worried one of Munders's thugs might use him as target practice. But Josh had wanted to sit where he could watch the street, see Munders coming.

They had compromised with a table inside by the window. Josh had promised Serena he'd keep a sharp lookout for any signs of a sniper.

The park was directly across the street, the trees thinned of their leaves on this hot summer day, and the low-lying rooftop of the redbrick building kitty-corner of the coffee shop was in plain view. A shooter would be easy to spot. So far, everything looked clear.

"Would you like a warm-up?"

Josh turned to the waitress standing beside the table holding a coffeepot. He slid his cup over. "Sure."

She poured more of the dark French roast into the cup. The delicious smell of the bean rose in the air.

The bell over the door chimed.

His pulse spiked. He glanced up, expecting to see

a short, gray-haired man. The photos they had of Fred Munders had been grainy and taken from a distance, but Josh was sure he'd recognize the lawyer on sight.

A woman pushing a stroller entered the coffeehouse.

Disappointment rushed through Josh. He picked up the coffee mug and blew on the steaming liquid before sipping the tasty brew.

Growing more impatient, he glanced at his watch again. "It's nearly ten-thirty. He's not going to show."

Serena heaved a sigh.

Josh wasn't sure if it was with relief or disappointment.

"I think you're right. Let's wrap up this operation," she said. He watched her slide out of the booth and walk toward the door. They'd worn their Jack and Susan Andrews outfits. Josh appreciated the way the hem of her skirt swirled around her knees when she walked. He watched the gentle sway of her hips as she left the coffee shop and headed down the street. He would miss seeing her in dresses every day when they went back to their regular jobs. He'd miss the affection and the companionship, as well.

"I'll meet you around back at the SUV," he said softly before taking one last swig from the coffee cup. He then laid down enough cash to cover the coffee and a healthy tip before heading out the door.

When he reached the SUV, Serena was in the passenger seat with a cell phone pressed to her ear. "Really? That's fabulous. We'll be there as soon as we can. Please keep this to yourself for now. I'll explain when we get there."

She hung up. Excitement fairly radiated from her. "That was the St. Louis crime lab. They've isolated another voice on the message Daniel left. The tech said there are one or two audible words."

Josh's stomach clenched. They both had so much hope

riding on recognizing the voice. But what if they couldn't? The disappointment would be a blow.

"We're going to Munders first," he said. "Call the chief and let him know."

"On it."

While she made the call, Josh maneuvered the Suburban through the midmorning traffic of downtown St. Louis. The area was an eclectic mix of modern and historic architecture, some dating back as far as the late 1800s. Munders's law firm resided in a more modern skyscraper.

They met the chief, Agent Bishop and the attorney general at the nearest intersection. A team of agents comprised of U.S. marshals and FBI agents were preparing to breach the building. Josh parked the SUV. Then he and Serena joined the others.

Burke Trier slapped him on the back. "Glad you could join us."

"Yeah, wouldn't miss it for the world," Josh replied. He wished his team leader, Hunter Davis, could be in on taking down Munders. But he and his new bride were in hiding from Munders's men, waiting for the day when it would be safe for them to return to St. Louis.

Glancing around, Josh asked, "Where's Bud?"

"Called in sick," Burke said with a shake of his head. "The man eats way too many carbs and enough fats to choke a horse. I'd be sick, too, if I ate like that." He shuddered. "I'll be glad when he decides to really retire. I'm tired of my car always smelling like fast food."

Josh didn't envy Burke his assignment of partnering with Bud. As a consultant, Bud's authority went only so far. He needed to be with an active-duty marshal when out in the field. Josh was thankful the chief had partnered him with Serena. Their time together had started out tense, but ever since she'd listened to Daniel's message, her attitude toward Josh had noticeably shifted.

Her words came back to him, each phrase like a stone in a tumbler, knocking against each other until their meaning gleamed like polished gems: *At some point you'll have to forgive yourself. Or you'll always be burdened by unnecessary guilt. You can regret not picking up the phone, but you don't get to feel guilty for his death.*

"We have men stationed at every exit point," the chief said, jerking Josh's thoughts back to the moment at hand.

"I want this handled properly," the attorney general said while mopping his brow with a handkerchief. "We can't have any mistakes. This case is barely holding together as it is."

"Yes, sir," Josh replied as he donned a flak vest with the U.S. Marshals Service seal emblazoned on the front.

Serena put one on, as well. The vest looked out of place with the summer dress she wore. Her nervousness showed in the rapid beat of her pulse beneath her creamy skin, and it distracted him. He wanted to kiss away her anxiety, to take her in his arms and let her know he'd protect her with his life.

Agent Bishop cleared his throat.

Josh jerked his gaze away from his pretend wife and met the agent's knowing gaze. Clamping down his attraction to Serena, Josh said, "Do we have a floor plan for the offices?"

Bishop nodded and led them to the back of a dark-colored van. He unrolled the fourth-floor blueprints. "This is Munders's law firm." He pointed to the far corner office. "We believe this is Fred Munders's office."

Josh would head straight there. He wanted to be the one to arrest Fred Munders. He wanted closure on this case so they could concentrate on Daniel's murder. "We're set. Let's do this."

They took the elevator to the fourth floor. When they stepped out, the place was deserted. No one manned the reception desk. The company's logo was no longer hanging on the wall. Chunks of plaster showed evidence that the sign had been forcibly removed. Josh's stomach plummeted.

They fanned out. Josh and Serena headed toward the far end of the hall, where the biggest office was located. Along the hallway all the offices were vacant. No people. No paperwork. Only desks and empty filing cabinets. Not even a stapler had been left behind.

With each step, anger tightened a knot in Josh's chest. The rats had abandoned ship.

They reached the corner office and pushed open the door. It, too, was devoid of anything but a desk, a chair and a credenza with its empty drawers open, taunting Josh. He let out a roar of frustration. He wanted to pick the chair up and throw it out the window. He shoved his weapon into its holster.

"Someone tipped them off." Serena's calm voice brought Josh back from the edge.

Making a fist, Josh said, "Let's get out of here."

When they were reassembled outside, Josh turned to the chief. "Who knew about this raid?"

"Only the people here. We've been planning this all morning, no one has been out of our sight. But Munders couldn't have evacuated the whole floor in that short amount of time. This was done before today, like he anticipated that raiding his offices was our next move."

"Yeah. He probably had someone watching Eve Cardinalli's house. When we showed up there, he must have gotten spooked."

"But we went there dressed as Jack and Susan," Serena said with a pensive frown. "No way could anyone have known we were marshals unless they actually knew us."

"The intruders you shot last night have been in isolation since being taken into custody," the chief said. "Neither is talking."

"Which leads us back to the leak in the department," Josh said. "But who? We've been so careful."

"Maybe the leak came from within the FBI and not the Marshals Service," Serena offered.

"Hey, it's not coming out of my office," Bishop insisted. "Only two people know about this operation. Me and my boss."

"As much as I hate thinking that someone we work with is dirty," Josh said. "There hadn't been a fed in the Marshals Service office at the time when Dylan McIntyre's flash drive disappeared off my desk. No, the leak is one of our own. Whoever it is discovered what we were up to and gave Munders the heads-up."

"What about the adoption agency?" Serena questioned.

Josh met her gaze and saw the same suspicion in her eyes that was curling through him. "We'd better get over there."

The chief gave the order to move the operation to the Perfect Family Adoption Agency. When they arrived at the brick building, the front door was ajar. Inside, it was empty and cleaned out, just like the law firm's offices.

Standing in the reception area, Josh turned to the chief. "This isn't good. They could be out of the country by now."

With his phone in his hand, Agent Bishop said, "I'm sending agents to the airport, train station and bus depot."

"Burke!" the chief called. "Have the local police put out a Be On the Look Out order for Fred Munders and his wife."

"Yes, sir," Burke said.

"And get me a list of the employees from both the law

firm and this place," the chief growled. "Someone's got to know where the Munderses have gone."

Noting Serena had disappeared down the hall, Josh went in search of her and found her standing inside Mrs. Munders's office. The place was a disaster, with empty file folders strewn about the floor, drawers hanging open and the walls barren.

Serena stood in front of the blank spot where the collage of babies had hung. She glanced at him, her eyes teary.

"We'll never know where those babies came from or who they really belong to," she said, her voice thick with emotion.

His heart in his throat, he pulled her into his arms.

She willingly went, her whole body melting against him. She laid her cheek on his chest.

He was sure she could feel the thudding of his heart. He rubbed small circles on her back. "We'll find the babies and their mothers. We'll make this right, somehow."

"I hope so. I can't help but think there are more young mothers like Lonnie who felt trapped and are being intimidated into giving up their children."

"Let's concentrate on finding the Munderses," Josh said. "They have the answers we need."

They stood silent for a moment. With a start, he realized he was gently rocking her back and forth. He stilled, and would have stepped away but her arms tightened around him.

"I want to put this behind us so we can concentrate on finding Daniel's killer."

A spasm of pain slashed through Josh. "We're closer than we were. As soon as we can, let's head to the crime lab to see what they discovered."

Leaning back to look up at him, Serena's brown eyes

regarded him steadily. "Promise me we won't stop looking for the person who murdered my brother."

"I promise." He'd let the investigation stagnate for too long while working on bringing down the illegal adoption ring.

Burke ran into the office. "Hey—"

Serena jerked out of Josh's arms. Reluctantly, he dropped his arms to his sides and stepped back.

Burke's eyebrows shot upward. "O-kay. I see how it is."

"You don't see anything," Josh growled. "What did you want?"

With a smirk, Burke said, "Right." He gestured with his head. "The chief wants you."

Serena walked past Burke, her head held high and her cheeks pink. Josh followed.

Burke fell into step beside him and elbowed him in the ribs. "So? You're sweet on Summers, huh?"

"Can it," Josh snapped.

Burke chuckled. "Hey, man, I don't blame you. She's a looker. A little too uptight for my tastes, but hey—" He shrugged.

Anger flooded Josh, but he refrained from biting Burke's head off. This was neither the time nor the place to deal with Burke's opinion of Serena. He picked up the pace and headed outside where the chief, Agent Bishop and Serena waited.

"SLMPD says there's activity at the Munderses' house," the chief said. "I want you three to head over there. See if you can find out where the Munderses have gone."

Maybe they hadn't lost the Munderses' trail, after all. This wasn't over yet. There was still a chance to bring Fred and Matilda Munders to justice and save innocent lives.

But ending the one would also put an end to the charade of a marriage between him and Serena.

* * *

Serena climbed out of the SUV and stared at the stately 1900s home of Fred and Matilda Munders. The large red-brick and stonework house had ornate gables, dormer windows in a mix of historic styles. A wide walkway led to the oversize front door.

Behind her, Burke and Josh climbed out of the vehicle and joined her on the porch. She was glad the chief had instructed Burke to join them. His presence kept the conversation limited to the case, since the love she harbored for Josh was too new, too raw, for her to deal with yet.

Well, at least she and Burke had talked about the case while Josh contributed a few grunts.

She understood his brooding mood. He was anxious to bring Munders in. He'd anticipated the meeting today being the nail in the proverbial coffin. But with Fred Munders in the wind their chances of bringing him to justice were dwindling. They had to find him and Matilda before they left the country.

Serena hoped the house staff, and she had no doubt there were some, knew where their employers would go.

They approached the door. Josh banged the large gold door knocker. The metal-on-metal sound bounced off the cavernous stone porch.

A moment later Matilda Munders opened the door. Her normally coiffed hair was mussed and her face devoid of makeup. She was wearing a yellow housecoat and slippers. She blinked at them. "Jeannie?" A huge smile broke out on her wrinkled face. She opened her arms to Serena. "Darling, you've come home."

Serena threw Josh a panicked glance before Matilda enveloped her in a warm hug. The woman felt fragile in Serena's arms. She patted the woman's back.

"Uh, Mrs. Munders," Serena said after a long moment.

Matilda pulled away to stare at Serena. Confusion clouded Matilda's eyes. "Oh, my. You're not my Jeannie."

Feeling sorry for the older woman, Serena smiled. "No, I'm not."

Matilda's gaze bounced to Josh then to Burke then back to Serena. "I know you. Susan, right?"

"Yes." Seemed easiest to go with her undercover identity than to try to explain who she really was. "Mrs. Munders, where is your husband?"

"Fred is on his way home. We're leaving." Matilda's eyes widened. "Oh, no. I'm not ready. He said to be ready at noon." Her gaze darted to the large, ornately carved grandfather clock dominating the entryway. "He'll be here soon. I must dress." She shuffled away toward the grand staircase.

"Wait a minute," Burke said, bustling forward. "We have to take her into custody."

Josh put a restraining hand on him. "Let Serena take care of her."

Touched by Josh's consideration of Matilda's modesty, Serena followed Matilda upstairs. She wouldn't take Mrs. Munders into custody in her robe and slippers. Behind her, Serena heard Josh and Burke arguing.

Moving boxes filled the bedroom. The bed was stripped; the cupboards of the beautiful armoire that Matilda stood in front of were empty. Empathy twisted in Serena's chest at the confused look on the older woman's face.

"I don't know where my clothes went," Matilda said, her voice small. "Clarice took them away."

"Clarice?" Serena asked gently.

Matilda whirled around as if only realizing now that Serena had followed her into the bedroom. "Oh, goodness, you're still here." She went to a box and ripped open the tape and started flinging clothes out. "Clarice is our housekeeper, but Fred fired her this morning. He fired everyone this morning. Then he left."

"Do you know where he went?"

Matilda waved a hand in the air. "I'm not his keeper. He'll be back when he's back. Then we'll go."

"Where are you going?"

The older woman tilted her head to the side. "I don't know. Fred didn't say. Only that we had to leave right away."

"Do you know why you have to leave?"

Clutching a shirt to her chest, she frowned. "I— No. Susan, what are you doing here? Did we have an appointment?"

"Mrs. Munders, my name isn't Susan Andrews. I'm U.S. Marshal Serena Summers."

Matilda's gaze narrowed on Serena. "Marshal?" She backed up a step, her eyes widening. "Fred said the marshals were after him. What have you done with my husband?"

Holding up a hand, Serena strove to calm the older woman. "We have done nothing with your husband. We're looking for him. Do you know where he is?"

"Why? What do you want with him?"

"Mrs. Munders, do you know where the babies that you place come from?"

"From mothers who don't want them," she replied, her tone suggesting that Serena should know the answer. "I make sure the wee ones have good homes with people who will provide a better life for them."

"Have you met the birth mothers?"

Matilda took an armful of clothes and headed toward the bathroom to change. "That's Fred's job. I meet with prospective families." She paused. "He gave me a purpose after my Jeannie died. I help others have what I lost." With that she went into the bathroom and slammed the door closed.

Just as Serena had thought. Fred was behind the adoption scam. But that didn't give Matilda a free pass. Now if they could find Fred, then justice would be served, and she and Josh could concentrate on finding her brother's killer. And then?

She and Josh would have to figure out their future.

THIRTEEN

"Where's Mrs. Munders?" Josh asked Serena when he stepped into the Munderses' master bedroom. He wasn't surprised to see the packing boxes stacked around. The rest of the house showed signs of moving, as well. The Munderses had had a busy weekend.

After Serena and Mrs. Munders had gone upstairs, Josh had searched the house in case Fred Munders was hiding. Unfortunately, he was nowhere to be found. He'd left his wife alone, unprotected. Why Josh was surprised by that he couldn't say.

Serena stood at the window overlooking the street. She pointed to a closed door on his left. "She's changing her clothes."

"Did she tell you where her husband went?"

"No. But she knows we're after him."

Figures. Frustration tensed the muscles in his neck. The department leak had given Munders a heads-up. "Does she know where they are going?"

"Not that I can tell. But she confirmed Fred is the mastermind. He brings her the babies. She claims she'd never met any of the children's mothers. She truly believes she's doing a good deed by finding the babies homes with adoptive parents."

"Doesn't matter what she believes," Josh stated. "Police officers are here to take her into custody."

Serena nodded and walked to the closed door. Knocking softly, she said, "Mrs. Munders, we need you to come out now."

No response.

Josh moved closer, concerned that the woman might have done something to herself. If she realized they were there to arrest her, she might hurt herself to get out of going to jail. From the troubled frown marring Serena's brow, she, too, was fearful of what Mrs. Munders might do. Serena banged louder on the door. "Mrs. Munders? Matilda?"

The door swung open. Serena and Josh jumped back. Josh's hand rested on the butt of his gun. He wasn't sure what to expect from Mrs. Munders. If she went psycho on them, he wanted to be ready. He caught the chiding look Serena sent his way and shrugged.

Matilda blinked at them, clearly startled to see them. She swept past them wearing a purple silk blouse and a flowered skirt. She'd brushed her hair and applied a touch of makeup. She appeared more like the woman they'd come to know at the adoption agency. "I wasn't expecting to see you today. I'm going on a trip with my husband. Have you seen him? Have you seen Fred?"

Josh arched an eyebrow. "Mrs. Munders, we need to take you downtown."

Serena edged closer, holding out a hand. "We'll help you find your husband."

Matilda smiled fondly at Serena and slipped her hand into Serena's. "Thank you, Jeannie. You're such a sweet girl."

They led Mrs. Munders downstairs and outside, where St. Louis police officers waited to take her into custody.

Burke pointed to Mrs. Munders and barked, "Arrest that woman."

Matilda halted and snatched her hand back from Serena. "I don't understand." Her voice shook, her eyes widened with fear. "What's happening?" She whirled to face Serena. "Susan? Susan, please tell me what's happening. Where's Fred?"

Josh's heart twisted at the look of empathy on Serena's face as she tried to soothe the older woman's fears.

"I'm Marshal Summers, remember?" Serena took her hand again. "Everything will be all right, Mrs. Munders. These men will take you someplace safe."

"But I don't understand. I haven't done anything wrong," Matilda insisted. She resisted going with the officers as they tried propelling her toward the waiting cruiser.

"Some of the infants your husband found for you weren't given freely. They were taken illegally," Serena explained.

"But I gave them good homes. Better homes than they would have had. Why am I being punished for that?" Tears rolled down Matilda's cheeks.

When one of the officers placed handcuffs around Matilda's wrists, Serena protested. "Are those really necessary?"

The officer hesitated as if assessing the threat Matilda presented, then apparently deciding the cuffs weren't required, he removed them.

Josh cupped Serena's elbow and tugged her back. "Let them do their jobs."

"Did she tell you where to find her husband?" Burke asked Serena.

"No. She doesn't know. He's supposed to be here at noon to pick her up."

"Then we'd better stay put," Burke stated, crossing his arms over his chest. "In case he shows."

"Good idea," Josh said, though he doubted Fred would show. The leak would most likely tell him they had taken his wife into custody. "You stay. We have somewhere we have to be."

He met Serena's gaze. As quickly as a question formed in her eyes, dawning realization had her mouthing an *oh* with an eager nod. They needed to go to the crime lab to hear the cleaned-up audio from Daniel's message. Her grateful smile smacked into him like a right cross. They moved in tandem at a brisk pace toward the SUV.

"What?" Burke sputtered. "You're going to leave me here alone?"

"Not alone," Josh replied over his shoulder. "You'll have SLMPD to watch your back."

"Where are you going?" Burke demanded.

Josh opened the passenger door for Serena and waited for her to climb in before shutting the door and rounding the front end. Before sliding into the driver's seat, he called out, "Let me know if Munders shows."

"I feel bad for Mrs. Munders."

Josh gave Serena a sideways glance. "You going soft on me, Summers?"

"I know I shouldn't. The woman's up to her neck in the illegal activities and has to be held accountable for the wrong she's done, but I can't help thinking her mind is not operating at full speed."

"I wondered if the diminished capacity was more than mere old-age-induced dementia."

"That's what I'm thinking," Serena said. "Because she's not that old. It could be early-onset Alzheimer's."

"Call the chief. Fill him in on her status."

"Good idea." The pleased note in her voice warmed him.

When they arrived at the St. Louis forensic crime lab,

all thoughts of the Munderses left Josh as anticipation knotted in his chest. He sent up a silent prayer that whatever they heard on the tape would be the key to finding Daniel's murderer. They headed to the fourth floor of the St. Louis Metropolitan Police Department, where the new thirty-thousand-square-foot crime lab had recently been completed, making the state-of-the-art forensic unit the most sophisticated in Missouri.

They met the deputy director of the lab, Maria Sanchez, a pretty woman in her forties. She escorted them past large cubicles where machines hummed and technicians studied various pieces of evidence. None of the techs seemed to notice them; each was intent on the work before them. Josh figured it took a certain kind of person to be willingly trapped inside a lab for hours on end studying a variety of substances collected at crime scenes. He much preferred to be out in the field.

Maria led them to an office in the corner. High-end recording and editing equipment filled the room.

"Colin, this is U.S. Marshals McCall and Summers. Colin O'Riley is our chief technical engineer," Maria explained before walking away.

Of medium height and build, with thick glasses and a white technician's lab coat, Colin shot them a quick smile of greeting. "I was hoping you'd show up soon. I'm about to go on vacation. My kids are chomping at the bit. We're heading to Disney World."

"Tell us what you have and we'll let you get on your way," Josh said, as anxious to get down to business as O'Riley seemed to be.

Colin moved to one of the machines. "I've cleaned up the sound quality on the recording as best I could and isolated the section in question." He flipped some switches and fiddled with a dial. "Here we go."

Josh flinched, just as he had the last two times he heard

the message. Serena threaded her fingers through his. Her words reverberated through his mind: *At some point you'll have to forgive yourself. Or you'll always be burdened by unnecessary guilt.*

But it wasn't unnecessary. Or was it?

Colin stopped the tape. "This is the section you wanted enhanced. I've done what I could. I'll turn up the volume, but you'll still have to listen closely."

The scuffling noise of Daniel adjusting the phone and covering the phone's mic with his hand filled the room. The muffled timbre of Daniel's words weren't clear. Then just muffled silence. No, wait. Josh clearly heard something.

"Play that back," Serena said. Obviously, she'd heard it, too.

Colin smiled. "You caught that. Good." He rewound the message. Stopped, then hit Play.

Josh strained to make out the voice of the other person. Closing his eyes, he concentrated on listening. The words *come* and *with* were barely audible. Something tugged at him, as if he should know that voice.

"'Come with,'" Serena said. "I definitely heard the words 'come with.'"

Josh nodded. "Me, too."

"Does the voice sound familiar to either of you?" Colin asked.

"Maybe," Josh said, searching his memory for something to indicate who the voice belonged to, but nothing solidified. "I don't know."

"Same here," Serena said, frustration flashing in her brown eyes. "It's like I should know who that is, but yet it's not distinct enough for me to really hear the voice. Does that make sense?"

"Yes." Josh turned to Colin. "There's no way to make the voice clearer?"

"Like I said, I've done what I could." Impatience threaded through Colin's voice. "Do you need to hear it again, or are we done?"

Josh didn't need to have the message repeated, didn't want to feel the slicing guilt again at hearing Daniel's voice, or his request for help. "Can you play that one section over?"

Colin did. The voice still proved elusive to Josh's memory banks. Irritated with himself, he turned to Serena. She was watching him with a look in her eyes that made his heart thump. "What? Did you recognize the voice?"

"No. Unfortunately." She turned to Colin. "I want a copy of that section but nothing else." Glancing at Josh, she said, "Maybe someone else in the department will recognize the voice."

"Good idea." Respect and admiration for Serena rushed through Josh. She wanted to see if anyone knew that voice, yet she wanted to protect him and Daniel.

They took the copy of the recording and left the crime lab. Once they were in the car, Josh drove to the Marshals Service building, one of the tallest structures in the city.

As he parked by the elevator his cell phone rang. He checked the caller ID. Munders! His heart sped up. He tapped Serena's knee as he pressed the answer button and then put the phone on speaker. "Jack Andrews."

"Give it up, Marshal McCall," Munders gravelly voice came out of the little device. "I know who you are."

Josh blinked. The traitor in the department was letting it all fly. "Then you know we have your wife in custody," Josh stated. "Give yourself up, Munders. You're done. There will be no more illegal adoptions."

"You need to let my wife go!" Munders cried. "She's not involved in this."

"But she is," Josh countered. "She brokered the adoptions. Adoptions of infants you stole from their mothers."

"She didn't know," Munders insisted. "She has the beginning stages of Alzheimer's. She can't be held responsible."

Josh exchanged a glance with Serena. From her expression, he could tell she thought that made sense.

"The only way she'll get leniency is if you give yourself up," Josh said. "And give us the names of all your underlings and the records of all the babies you've stolen."

"I'm not the one in charge," Munders stated. "I only do what I'm told. If you want to know who's behind the illegal adoptions then come to the Arch at noon."

The line went dead.

"Isn't Congressman Peter Simms holding a press conference at the Arch to announce his candidacy?" Serena asked.

Glancing at his watch, Josh nodded. "Yep. In fifteen minutes." He handed her his phone. "Call the chief. Let him know about this latest development." Josh started the SUV. Checking to see if anyone recognized the voice on the tape would have to wait.

"Do you think Munders is hinting that the congressman is the one behind the illegal adoption ring?" Serena asked, rebuckling her seat belt.

"I don't know, but I intend to find out."

Heart pounding with anticipation, Serena followed on Josh's heels as they threaded their way single file through the crowd gathering on the lawn beneath the famed and iconic monument symbolizing the westward expansion of the United States: the Gateway Arch.

Serena had visited the site as a kid with her grade school class and as an adult once with Daniel. She'd stood beneath the steel structure, marveling at the grandeur of the architectural wonder and feeling patriotic. Today, however, her focus was on Peter Simms. And how he might play into the illegal adoption ring.

There was no mistaking the tall, elegant, black-haired man wearing a tailored navy suit and red tie taking the podium beneath an arch of red, white and blue balloons waving merrily in the noon breeze.

The crowd cheered. The congressman raised a hand.

Keeping her weapon concealed in the folds of her skirt, Serena searched the audience, spotting several plain-clothed officers and three U.S. marshals sent by the chief. They formed a perimeter around the gathering; each held a photo of Fred Munders.

For a moment a familiar face appeared near the podium. Serena grabbed Josh's sleeve. "Hey, Bud's here, near the platform."

Josh stretched to see over the heads of the many people congregating on the lawn. "Where? I don't see him."

Serena didn't now, either. "I'm sure it was him, wearing a light-colored polo shirt, khaki pants and a Cardinals baseball cap. I thought he'd called in sick."

"That's what Burke said." Josh grabbed her hand. "Come on, let's get closer."

On the dais, Simms began his speech. "Thank you, good citizens of St. Louis and the great state of Missouri. What a great turnout."

People clapped. Photographers snapped photos. Energy charged the air. Serena concentrated on the sea of faces, looking for Mr. Munders.

"We gather here today out of love for our state, for our country. We gather here today out of concern for our country." Simms smiled wide, his bright blue gaze grazing over the audience. "We have an opportunity today to effect some change. Our country is in turmoil. We need new leadership." A roar of agreement went up from the crowd. After a beat, Simms said, "I am going to be that leader. I'm announcing my bid for the office of president of the United States."

A cheer erupted.

"Tell the people how you got your funding!" A loud, gravelly voice yelled from somewhere to Serena's right.

Josh froze.

Serena bumped against him. She scanned the crowd.

Catching sight of the lawyer, Serena pointed. "Josh, it's Munders! See him? In the gray suit and the tortoise-shell glasses."

Josh tugged her forward. They pushed through the crowd. Josh yelled, "Move, U.S. Marshals!"

People scattered. Serena kept her gaze on Munders as he weaved and bobbed, evading capture as officers moved in on him.

Simms quickly grabbed the nearest officer, though the mic picked up his words. "That man is wanted by the U.S. Marshals. He's crazy. You have to stop him."

"Don't believe him!" Munders shouted. "He's covering up murder and corruption!" He turned and ran for the visitors' center.

Serena and Josh chased after Munders, leaving behind the buzz of reporters and photographers swarming the congressman. Serena knew others would take Simms statement and investigate Munders's allegations.

"The tram!" Serena pointed to a staircase down which Munders had disappeared. The staircase led to the tram that conveyed passengers to the uppermost part of the arch.

They raced down the stairs.

"Move, move!" Josh instructed the throng of people coming and going from the tram.

"Munders, halt!" Josh shouted.

Munders skidded to a stop in front of a tram door for the south leg and whirled around. He held a weapon.

"Gun!" Serena shouted.

Screams echoed in the cavernous arch lobby. People scattered, some crouching to make themselves smaller targets.

The tram doors to the south leg of the arch slid open. A family of four tried to leave the pod. Munders pushed them back in, holding them at gunpoint until the door slid shut. The tram on the north leg had an out-of-service sign taped to the doors.

"I'll take the stairs, you jump in that capsule," Josh instructed, pointing to the next open pod on the tram.

"Josh, there are over a thousand steps," Serena said, remembering being impressed by the number when she was a kid. "He'll be back down before you reach the top."

Gripping her by the elbow, he shoved her into the egg-shaped pod. She ducked to keep from hitting her head. "I'll meet you up there."

The doors slid shut. Alone inside the small, white capsule, Serena was forced to sit as the tram inched its way up to the highest peak of the arch. The swaying motion of the car made her stomach churn. Every nerve in her body throbbed with anticipation and anxiety.

What would Munders do? Would she and Josh be able to disarm him before he hurt anyone?

When she reached the pinnacle of the arch, the door slid open just as an emergency alarm echoed off the steel walls. The tram doors locked in the open position.

Cautiously, Serena stepped out, her weapon at the ready. She waved startled civilians out of the way.

Having released the family trapped in the pod with him, Fred Munders pushed through the other visitors, clearly looking for an escape in the seven-foot-wide landing. The observation windows were only seven by twenty-seven inches, not large enough to squeeze through and hurl himself, or anyone else, to their death.

He saw Serena and his gaze narrowed. He grabbed the nearest woman, an older lady with short curly hair, dressed in Bermuda shorts and a print blouse. She shrieked as he dragged her in front of him, using her as a shield. He held the gun to the woman's head. "Lay down your weapon!"

The hostage's pale blue eyes pleaded with Serena to protect her. Knowing she had backup on the way, Serena lowered the gun to the ground and then held up her hands. She had to defuse the situation. She couldn't let a civilian get hurt. "You don't want to do this, Mr. Munders. Matilda needs you."

"She's not involved!" he shouted. "Get this tram going again!"

Knowing she had to talk him down, Serena strove to keep her voice even, nonthreatening. "I can't. There's no way out, Fred. Let me help you."

He scoffed. "Help me? You want to put me away for things I didn't do."

Reining in anger and disgust that even now he would deny his culpability, she said, "Then who? Congressman Simms?"

A door at the far end of the observation deck slid open. Josh stepped out, his chest heaving with exertion, but the gun he aimed at Munders was rock steady. Munders swung his weapon toward Josh. "Hold it. Don't make a move or I'll blow your head off."

Serena's throat constricted. She inched forward. If she could get close enough, she could disarm Munders.

Josh held up his hands in entreaty. "No one wants to get hurt, Fred."

"You should have left well enough alone," Fred shouted. "And if your nosy buddy had done the same, he'd still be alive!"

Serena froze. Shock tore through her. She met Josh's startled gaze.

"Who are you talking about?" Josh asked.

Fred dragged his hostage backward until his back was at the wall. He swept the weapon back and forth between Josh and Serena, before coming to a halt at the base of his hostage's head. "Your dead partner, Marshal McCall."

FOURTEEN

Josh's heart clawed into his throat. Munders murdered Daniel? How else would Munders know they had been partners? It was too surreal. All this time they'd been trying to bring the man to justice for an entirely different reason, not knowing he was the one who'd killed Serena's brother.

"You killed Daniel?"

The shock and rage in Serena's voice threaded through Josh, wrapping around his heart like packing tape.

Fred shifted slightly to face Serena, the gun in his hand aimed at the woman held captive in his arms. The woman had her eyes squeezed closed and her lips moved with silent words.

"Whoa! I didn't say that!" Fred cried. "You can't pin his murder on me."

"Then who?" she demanded, stepping forward; the intense blaze in her brown eyes should have burned Munders to ash.

Josh used the distraction Serena provided to edge closer to Munders.

"Not so quick, missy!" Fred shouted, wildly waving the gun in his hand.

Onlookers screamed. Some hit the deck. Josh froze, afraid Munders would shoot an innocent bystander.

"If you want to know who killed your brother," Fred continued, "then make me a deal."

Frustration flared in her expression. "You know I don't have the authority to do that. The only way you'll get a deal is if you release the hostage and come with us peacefully."

Josh inched another foot toward Munders.

"You bring the AG here," Munders countered. "When I hear him say the words then I'll tell you what you want to know."

"The attorney general isn't coming up here, Fred," Serena said. "What about Matilda? Your wife doesn't understand what's happening. She deserves to know why she's going to jail."

Fred's face crumbled with pain and guilt. "I should have sent her away sooner. But she's lost without me." His expression hardened. "Don't you hurt her!"

Josh met Serena's gaze. He willed her to keep him distracted.

Serena held up her hands, palms out. "No one wants to hurt Matilda. She's a sweet lady who's been caught up in your mess. You need to do the right thing by your wife. Turn yourself in, face what you have done."

Josh closed in on the older man's position. Another foot and he'd be close enough to grab him.

Munders must have sensed the movement. He whirled toward Josh, the gun aimed at his heart. "Not another step, Marshal."

The hostage in Munders's clutches whimpered, and the terror in her wide eyes ripped through Josh's chest.

"Fred!" Serena's sharp, fear-filled voice bounced against the steel walls. "Matilda needs you."

Keeping his gaze on the weapon aimed at him, Josh said, "Think of your wife, man. If you shoot me, you'll get the death penalty. Then what would happen to her?"

"She loves you, Fred," Serena said, her voice now soft and coaxing. "If you cooperate, you can see her. Help her to understand what's happening. She's scared and alone. You don't want her to face this by herself, do you?"

Indecision marched across Fred's face. He turned toward Serena, the weapon in his hand now aimed at Serena's heart. Josh's gut clenched. He couldn't let the man hurt Serena. From the moment he stepped out of the stairwell, when he'd seen Munders aiming his weapon at Serena, Josh's blood had run cold. If anything happened to her, he wouldn't be able to go on.

In that instant, a truth he'd been trying to deny slammed into him.

He loved Serena.

Acceptance of that fact slid into place like a puzzle piece that had been missing.

Sending up a silent plea of protection for the woman he loved, Josh launched himself at Munders, slamming him against the wall and knocking the gun out of his hand.

Serena rushed forward to kick the weapon aside.

Munders's head hit the wall. A loud groan escaped. He loosened his hold on the hostage in his arms.

The woman twisted away and ran into Serena's waiting arms. She hustled the woman a few feet away and worked to calm her.

Josh grabbed Munders, spun him around to face the wall and yanked his arms behind his back. He grabbed the zip ties from his pocket. With satisfaction, he secured Munders's wrists together.

Serena hurried over with her phone. "The arch employees are going to get the tram going again."

Josh stared at her, taking in her pale complexion, her wide brown eyes, and felt his heart expand, nearly exploding from his chest. There had been a moment when he'd thought Munders would hurt her, and everything inside Josh had rebelled. He'd have gladly traded his life for hers.

He reached out to smooth a hand over her cheek. "You're okay?"

She turned her cheek into his palm. "Yes." Her gaze held his. "I thought he was going to kill you. I couldn't have taken losing you, too."

Her words shuddered through Josh.

Did he dare hope that she returned his feelings? And if she did, what then?

He forced his heart and his head to stay on task.

Dropping his hand away, he said, "Let's get him out of here."

The St. Louis police station buzzed with activity. Serena wove her way through the officers in Josh's wake toward the hall where the interrogation rooms were located. Her heart still pounded in her chest like an over-revved engine. Deep, calming breaths hadn't helped. Nothing would until she knew who had murdered her brother and why.

Josh held Munders in a firm grip, having refused to allow anyone else to take custody of their suspect. Serena appreciated how much Josh wanted answers, too.

He had as much at stake as she did in hearing the details of her brother's death.

She sent up a silent plea that truth would set Josh free of the burden of guilt he unjustly carried. She prayed Josh would realize he wasn't to blame and allow his heart to open to her, to her love.

It had taken seeing him almost get killed for her to admit to herself how deeply her feelings for Josh went. Her love for him was solidly in place. Whatever the risks, or the costs, she wanted a life with him.

"Inside," Josh commanded Munders as they reached the open door of an interrogation room.

The chief stopped Serena with a hand on her shoulder when she would have followed Josh into the room. Stung, she turned her gaze on her superior. "I need to hear this."

Harrison nodded. "You can from here."

He gestured for her to join him and the police captain in a smaller room that had a two-way mirror looking into the interrogation room. The mirror separated her from the man who held the secrets to her brother's death. The police captain hit a switch, allowing them to listen in.

"You said I could see my wife," Munders complained. He slumped in the metal chair. The guard cut the zip ties before stepping back. Munders rubbed his wrists.

"In due time. First tell me what you know about Marshal Daniel Summers's murder." Josh loomed over Fred, his expression as hard as granite.

"I told you, I'm not talking until I have a deal." His arms resting on the table next to the yellow pad and pen, waiting for his confession, Munders glanced up at Josh. "You tell the attorney general that."

Josh threw a glance at the mirrored wall. Serena felt Josh's impatience all the way through her bones.

"Why isn't the AG here?" she asked Harrison.

"He's here talking to the congressman, hoping to clear up Munders's accusations."

"Then we need him to talk to Munders," Serena said, aware her voice had risen but helpless to control the frustration constricting her throat.

"I'll let Mr. Kannon know what's going on," the police captain said and left the room.

Inside the interrogation room, Josh said, "We have you on the illegal adoptions. Your signature is on the paperwork." He leaned in, planting his hands on the table. "Do yourself a favor and cooperate. It will go smoother for you and your wife."

"Where is she?" Munders asked. He swallowed, his

Adam's apple bobbing, as if he were finding it difficult to hold back his emotions.

"She's here, sitting in a jail cell." Josh straightened, his voice hardening. "Is that what you want for your wife? For her to rot in jail?"

"She didn't know," Munders insisted again. "She trusted me. She's sick." He splayed his hands, palms up, on the table. "Please, she shouldn't be punished for my actions."

Serena's heart twisted with something akin to empathy. It was obvious the man loved his wife. She tamped down any and all sympathy for the guy. He was a murderer. Though she doubted he'd bloodied his hands literally, he'd ordered the deaths of several witnesses. He knew something about Daniel's death. Her fingers curled into a fist.

She willed Josh to break Fred, to make him talk.

"Look, I want to help you," Josh said, his voice shifting to a persuading tone Serena had never heard him use. The sound raised gooseflesh of anticipation on her arms. "I want to help your wife. But I can't unless you tell me what you know."

Munders gave him a sly glance. "I know a lot. But I'm not talking until I have the deal in front of me."

Josh glanced once again in the direction of the two-way mirror, the intensity in his gaze conveying he clearly wanted some action.

The door to the interrogation room opened and the attorney general entered. Heavyset with the wide shoulders of a linebacker, Carl Kannon exuded a vitality that would have eclipsed most men. But not Josh. Next to Kannon, Josh was the epitome of calm, cool and collected.

To Serena, Josh was the center of the universe. The center of her universe. She prayed he could feel the power of her support through the glass.

"I hear you want a deal," Kannon intoned in a deep

bass voice. "The only deal I'll consider is taking the death penalty off the table."

Munders sputtered. "I didn't kill the marshal!"

"But you ordered the hit on several others," Kannon stated, clearly unimpressed with Fred's outburst.

A mulish expression settled on Munders's face. "You've got no proof."

Kannon smiled, the gesture unpleasant. "The congressman says there is proof."

Munders's eyes widened with fear. "No way. They are not pinning everything on me. This wasn't my idea. I just went along with it to make some extra cash and to give Matilda a reason to get up every day."

Serena leaned forward, nearly pressing her nose against the glass. Who were his accomplices? And if he wasn't the mastermind behind the illegal adoption ring, then who was? She knew their focus should be on identifying Mr. Big. If it wasn't Munders, then who?

Come on, Josh, she silently pleaded. *Find out about Daniel.*

"Who's *they?*" Josh asked.

Munders's gaze bounced between the two men. His shoulders slumped. Apparently realizing he was trapped good and well, he said, "No death penalty. And Matilda doesn't do time."

"No death penalty. And your wife is sent to minium security, where she will get proper medical care," Kannon said. "Now talk."

"Start with Daniel," Josh said.

Anticipation tightened the knot in Serena's chest.

Resignation showed in Munders's face. "I'll admit to being in on the illegal adoptions and the hiring of men to take out witnesses, but I had nothing to do with the marshal's death."

"You implied you know who killed him," Josh said through clenched teeth. "Who killed him and why?"

"I can tell you the why, but as to who did the deed, I can only guess."

Josh's hands bunched into fists at his sides. Serena wanted to reach through the glass and wrap her fingers around Munders's throat for dragging this out.

Just tell us what happened, already, her mind screamed.

After a tense moment of silence, Munders said, "A year and a half ago a guy who had gotten in too deep with a loan shark in town was offered a way out of his debt if he'd sell his kid, but the guy got cold feet and refused to sell the baby in the end."

"Delacorte," Josh breathed out the name.

Munders shrugged. "Yeah, the guy liked the long shots."

Though Josh couldn't see her, Serena nodded. That made sense. After Joe Delacorte had been murdered, they'd uncovered his secret life of gambling and the high amount of debt he owed. His wife, Angel, had arrived in time to see the killers. Joe had warned her to protect their daughter. In the end, he'd protected his baby girl, but his wife and daughter had had to go into witness protection.

"What does that have to do with Marshal Summers's murder?" Kannon snapped.

"The marshal was onto us," Munders said. "I can only think Delacorte had spilled to him what we were doing."

Serena sucked in a breath. Daniel had mentioned a call that he thought was something big. Her heart ached with grief and anger.

"You and the congressman?" Kannon clarified.

Munders nodded. "And his brother, Judge Simon Simms."

"So the three of you killed Marshal Summers," Josh said, his voice shaking with rage.

Munders shook his head. "I don't know who actually killed him. He was dead when I arrived."

"Explain," Josh barked.

Munders cringed against Josh's wrath. "I was supposed to pick up a baby. When I got there, the marshal was dead. I hightailed it out of there."

Josh scrubbed a hand over his face. "Who were you supposed to meet?"

"Delacorte was supposed to bring the kid in exchange for some cash. Then I'd take the baby and give it to Matilda to place with a family."

"Who had the cash?" Kannon asked.

"Simon."

The name reverberated through Serena. Judge Simon Simms. Was he the one who'd killed her brother?

"Tell me about the leak in the U.S. Marshals Service," Kannon said.

Munders scrunched up his nose. "I don't know. That was Simon Simms's doing."

Kannon shoved the pad of paper and pen toward the disgraced lawyer. "Write it all down. This is the only way you get any leniency. I want everything. The names of your thugs, the names of the women you terrorized into giving up their babies and the names of the families those babies went to."

Josh left the interrogation room as Munders began scribbling on the pad of paper. Serena and the chief rushed out of the side room and met him in the hall.

"Good job, McCall," Harrison said, slapping Josh on the back.

"We have to find the judge," Serena said. She wouldn't be satisfied until the man who'd killed her brother was brought to justice and put away in jail for the rest of his life.

Josh took her hand. "Yes, we will. However, I'm not sure I'm willing to take the word of Fred Munders. He could be casting blame on the judge and the congress-man to save his own skin. I want a chat with the congress-man. See what he has to say for himself." Josh glanced at the chief.

"Have at him," the chief said.

Serena blocked his path. "Let me."

Josh exchanged a quick glance with the chief. At the chief's nod, Josh stepped aside. "He's yours to question."

Pleased by Josh's willingness to let her do some of the heavy lifting, she gave him a quick smile before en-tering the interrogation room where Congressman Peter Simms waited.

He looked up when she entered. "Can I have some water?"

She inclined her head, knowing Josh and the chief were watching and would fulfill the request. "Some will be brought in."

She took the seat across from Peter. "How did a man with such a promising political career get involved in an illegal adoption ring and murder?"

Peter's blue eyes darkened. "I don't know anything about any murders or the adoption scam."

"Seriously? You're going to deny it?" Serena shook her head. "Fred Munders is in the next room spilling his guts. He says you and your brother are the ones behind the il-legal adoption scam."

"I didn't know anything about the illegal activity until it was too late," Peter said. "My brother—" He clamped his lips tightly together.

"Your brother?" she prompted, impatient to get the truth. When he didn't continue, she said, "Your politi-cal career is over. Now it's a question of how long you're going to jail for. Help yourself and tell us everything."

His lifted his chin. "I swear I wasn't involved."

She sent him a dubious look. "Look, Congressman, we

have men in custody eager to make a deal. We've got Fred Munders pointing to you and your brother. We have witnesses willing to testify. We have a paper trail that will lead straight to your door. Not to mention what we'll find when we run your financials. You're done. The sooner you cooperate the better it will be for you."

He seemed to weigh her words. Regret flashed in his eyes but was quickly shuttered behind a mask of poise. The ultimate politician. "I don't know anything about my brother's illegal activities. Simon poured money into my campaign. I didn't ask where the money was coming from. That's the only crime I'm guilty of."

"What about the death of U.S. marshal Daniel Summers?" Serena choked out.

Guilt flickered beneath the politician's stare. Serena slammed her hand on the table. "Answer me!"

Peter flinched. "You'll have to talk to Simon about that."

"You're confirming your brother is the one who killed Daniel?"

"I'm not confirming or denying anything, Marshal Summers," Peter said smoothly, recovering from his momentary bout of conscience. "It's up to you to find the culprit. If my brother is guilty, then he will have to pay for his crime."

Irritated by his evasive answer, she narrowed her gaze on the politician. "Who in the U.S. Marshals Service is working with your brother?"

Peter spread his hands wide. "I do not know. Honestly, I don't."

She studied his face, his eyes, looking for deceit and not finding any. Frustration pounded at her temples. She believed him.

She exited the room with purposeful steps. It was time to put an end to this. The judge would answer for his crimes.

* * *

"Good work, Josh," Hunter Davis's deep voice came over the phone line. Josh and Serena had returned to the Marshals Service office, along with their chief. Josh sat at his desk, his gaze landing on the other marshals in the office as they worked on their cases. Which one was the traitor? "You and Serena work well together," Hunter commented. "I'm proud of you both."

Pleased by his former team leader's praise, Josh sat straighter and said into the receiver, "We're not done. We still have to find the leak and arrest the judge. The chief is getting a warrant now so we can arrest the judge and search his office and home for evidence connecting him to the case. The AG is leery of taking the word of Munders or the congressman. Judge Simms has a powerful hold on the city government."

"It will be good to have this over," Hunter said. "Annie and I plan on returning when we can put this behind us."

"We'd love to have you back," Josh said, meaning it. His gaze snagged on Serena coming out of the women's restroom. Her eyes looked red and there was a grim set to her jaw. Hearing about her brother's death had hurt her. Just as it had Josh. But it also angered him. Daniel had had backup. Backup that betrayed him. Betrayed them all. They had to find the traitor in the department and stop him.

Josh ended his call with Hunter, promising to let him know as soon as the situation was resolved and it would be safe for him and Annie to return to St. Louis. Going to Serena's side, he said, "If you need some time, everyone will understand."

She shot him a hot look. "I'm seeing this through, Josh."

He smiled with approval. "I figured as much but thought I'd offer."

Her expression softened. She laid a hand on his arm. "You're a good man, Josh McCall."

Her words speared him, making him want to sweep her into his arms and confess his love. But that would be foolhardy. If they wanted to go back to being colleagues, a romance between them wouldn't be wise. "Let's see where we stand with the judge."

The speculation in her eyes spurred him into motion. He knew her well enough to know she could see through him, see the effect her words had on him. He led her to the chief's office.

Harrison wasn't alone. Kannon tipped his chin in acknowledgment as they entered. "We've got the warrant and the indictment. The judge should be at the courthouse."

Anticipation revved through Josh's blood. Time to put an end to this, once and for all.

FIFTEEN

Josh surveyed the empty room, his blood pressure sky-rocketing. They'd driven to the courthouse in the county seat of Clayton to find the judge's chambers empty. The desk was neat and tidy; gold-gilded books lined a built-in bookshelf, the judge's robe hung from a standing coatrack in the corner. But the judge was nowhere to be found.

Beside Josh, Serena growled, "Where is he?" She moved to the desk and began rifling through the drawers.

Josh whirled on the clerk who'd followed them into the empty office. "Is he in court?"

The clerk, Ian Parker, a thin man with thick glasses, shook his head. "No. The judge didn't show up today." He hurried to the desk to block Serena. "Hey, you can't do that."

"We have a warrant," Serena replied, bending to search for any hidden compartments in the sides of the desk.

Josh watched, knowing if there was something to find, she'd find it. She was one of the most capable women he knew. The more time he spent with her, the more he admired her. When she shook her head and stalked away from the desk with her hands balled at her sides, he blew out a breath of frustration.

Ian frowned. "You don't think anything bad has happened to the judge, do you?"

"Not yet," Serena muttered. The rage trembling in her tone made Josh slant her a quick glance. She had to hold it together. They were close to finding out the truth of her brother's murder. The judge had the answers they sought.

A sense of urgency crowded through the anger. The judge must know they were onto him. The leak in the department had likely already informed the judge and sent the man scurrying for cover. Josh's fingers curled. Where would he run? "Do you have the judge's home address?"

Ian eyed them with concern. "You *do* think something bad has happened to him." He pushed his glasses up with his index finger. "I was afraid something like this would happen one day. He gets all sorts of crazy hate mail. Criminals promising retribution, families of victims angry if they perceive he's been too lenient."

"The address," Josh snapped, not needing to hear about the judge's safety concerns. The man was a criminal himself.

Hurrying out of the chamber and back to his desk, Ian's fingers quickly flew over the computer keys and printed off the judge's home address. "I'm not going to get into trouble for this, am I?"

"No." Serena took the address from Ian's hand. "You should get a medal."

They left the courthouse. Josh drove as fast as he safely could to the address Ian had supplied. The Hampton Park home of Judge Simon Simms sat on nearly two acres of sprawling manicured lawns, a wide variety of trees and well-maintained flower beds.

Josh whistled as he brought the vehicle to a halt at the front entrance. The colonial house with its dormer windows, brick exterior and white shutters oozed luxury. No wonder the judge had resorted to an illegal activity. The upkeep alone of a place like this would have set the judge back the sum of Josh's salary. His heart cramped. Anger flooded him.

The judge and Munders were just like Josh's father. Only on a much grander scale. His father had acted self-ishly, robbing others to pay for his gambling habit. Judge Simms and Fred Munders dealt in the human trafficking of innocent lives so they could live the high life. They were cut from the same ilk. Men who wanted more than they could afford, regardless of who they hurt in the process.

Josh would make sure those involved would serve their time.

Serena was already out of the car before Josh turned off the engine. He jumped out and caught up to her as she stepped onto the porch. She jabbed a finger at the door-bell. Inside the sound of a loud chime echoed.

Almost immediately the door was jerked open. A tall, elegant man, dressed in a black suit and white dress shirt with a black tie, stood in the doorway. "Yes, can I help you?"

Serena flashed her badge at the man. Josh followed suit.

"Marshals Summers and McCall," Serena said in a no-nonsense tone. "Is Judge Simms home?"

The man bent forward to study their IDs. He straightened. "No. He is gone."

"Gone where?" Josh asked.

"I don't know. He and the missus left for an extended trip. I was not informed where they were going or when they would be back."

"And you are…?" Serena asked.

"Henry. I manage the house."

"Of course you do," Serena muttered.

"We have a warrant to search the house." Josh took the warrant out of his suit jacket breast pocket and handed it over.

Henry accepted the document and stepped aside so they

could enter. The vast entryway, done in marble and crown molding, had hallway shoots going deeper into the house. A large staircase curved upward to the second floor.

Serena stood in front of a huge portrait of the judge and his wife that hung on the wall next to the staircase. Felicia Simms looked regal seated on a fancy, old-fashioned red sofa, wearing a long formal black dress, her black hair swept back from her pretty, pale face.

Behind her stood Simon. At least twenty years her senior, the silver-streak-haired man wore a tux; his hand rested possessively on his wife's shoulder. The expression of superiority on his face churned Josh's gut. He wanted to rip the painting from the wall and burn it.

"Does the judge have a home office?" Serena asked.

"This way," Henry intoned and strode down one of the hallways, his clipped stride quick with efficiency.

Josh and Serena hurried after the houseman. At a set of double doors, Henry halted. "Please try not to disturb the room too much."

"Can't make any promises," Josh stated, moving past the man and flinging the doors wide. He stepped into a long room done in wood paneling with floor-to-ceiling bookshelves and a wall of windows overlooking the side garden.

A desk was situated at one end of the room while the other end had a sitting area. A box of expensive cigars sat on an end table. Josh's gut clenched. He remembered his father once bringing home a similar box of cigars, bragging to his ten-year-old son how much money the imported contraband was worth.

Even at that tender age, Josh had thought the expense excessive, but he'd loved his father and had tried to appear impressed. Now he felt sickened by the memory.

Turning his attention to the desk, he joined Serena in searching the drawers. Pulling out file after file, his heart rate sped up. The judge apparently kept all his illegal activities in his desk. But none of these files told them where the man had skipped off to.

Josh's gaze went to the trash can beneath the desk. He grabbed the round, black container and fished out a wad of shredded paper. He heaved a sigh. Then as quickly as he could, he started piecing the strips together on the desktop, something marshals were quite adept at when on the trail of a fleeing felon.

An itinerary. The judge and his wife were booked on a one-way flight to Dallas with a final destination of Morocco. A country that didn't have an extradition treaty with the United States. The plane was scheduled to take off in less than a half hour.

Excitement revved through his blood. "Serena! We have to get to the airport."

At the Lambert–St. Louis International Airport, Serena pushed her way through the travelers. Beside her, Josh kept a hand at the small of her back, his touch creating sparks that propelled her forward.

They were so close to losing the judge. The plane had been boarded and was about to pull away from the gate. Though marshals could apprehend the judge when the plane landed in Dallas, Serena wanted to be the one to bring him in.

She'd called the chief and he in turn had called the air traffic controllers, but the red tape necessary to ground a plane could take more time than they had.

At the gate, the attendant blocked them from running down the gangway. "Excuse me!"

Serena and Josh flashed their badges.

"You have a passenger on board who is a wanted criminal," Josh explained. "We need to get on the plane to take him into custody."

"The door's been sealed. I'll let the captain know." The attendant hurried to her console.

Taking that as a sign they were free to proceed, Serena raced down the compact corridor toward the plane's door with Josh hot on her heels. She skidded to a halt. Josh stopped next to her and banged on the door.

The sound of the door latch opening filled Serena with anticipation. The second the door swung wide, she pushed past the surprised attendant and entered the plane.

Serena paused in the aisle of the first-class cabin, her gaze raking over the twenty-four passengers, expecting the judge and his wife to be seated in the expensive seats.

"See him?" Josh asked from behind her.

"No. You?" Maybe they'd changed their appearance, like she and Josh had for their undercover assignment. She studied each face, hoping for a telltale sign that would indicate which of these people were the ones she sought, but didn't see what she was looking for.

"Let's check the coach cabin," Josh suggested with a gentle nudge.

Blowing out a breath, she made her way down the center aisle. When she reached the closed curtain separating the first-class cabin from the economy class, she yanked it aside. A few people let out startled gasps.

Serena's gaze zeroed in on two people, sitting on the left side, midway down the cabin. The judge and his wife. Serena's heart vaulted with triumph.

Josh cupped her elbow. "By the book, Serena."

Taking in a shuddering breath, she nodded. She wanted to wrap her fingers around the older man's neck and squeeze. She would have to settle for handcuffs around his wrists.

She advanced on him. "U.S. Marshals. Judge Simon Simms, we are taking you into custody."

Simms jumped to his feet in the aisle and backed up. Fear twisted his face as he frantically looked for an escape.

Satisfaction roared through Serena. He should be scared. There was nowhere for him to run to. And with the tight airport security, they were assured he had no weapon.

"Simon?" Felicia Simms gaped at her husband. "What's going on?"

"You have no right," the judge sputtered. "I'm an officer of the court. You will stand down!"

"I don't think so." Serena drew to a halt an inch from him. "You are a murderer."

He drew himself up. "That's absurd!"

"You killed my brother, Marshal Daniel Summers," she shot back.

Baring his teeth, he snarled, "You can't prove anything."

"We will. Now turn around," she barked as she unclipped a set of handcuffs from the flak vest she wore.

"I'll have your badge for this," the judge warned but did as instructed.

"Feel free to try." With a gratifying snap, Serena cuffed his wrists together. She met Josh's gaze, the tenderness she saw there threatening to unleash the floodgate of emotion she struggled to hold back.

Finally, they had the man responsible for her brother's death in custody. Finally, the nightmare was over.

She pushed Simms forward toward the front of the plane, forcing him to walk in front of her.

Josh leaned over to offer Mrs. Simms a hand. "You'll need to come with us as well, ma'am."

Serena steered the judge down the aisle. Something to her right caught her attention as she passed by. A red Cardinals baseball cap. Like the one she'd seen Bud Hollingsworth wearing at Congressman Simms's Gateway Arch appearance.

She stopped abruptly and turned around to stare. Josh bumped into her, his strong hands settling on her shoulders. The man in the window seat had the red cap pulled low, one hand up shielding the rest of his face, and his body angled way. Clearly he was trying not to be noticed. He had on a light-colored polo shirt and khaki pants.

"Serena, what's wrong?" Josh asked with concern in his tone.

"Bud," she said, pointing to the man she'd just passed, who hadn't moved a muscle.

Josh leaned across the passenger in the aisle seat to yank the baseball cap off the man's head.

It was Bud!

His hand fell to his lap and he straightened. "You've blown my cover."

Confused, Serena sought Josh's gaze. Cover?

"Explain yourself," Josh bit out to Bud.

"I've been tailing the judge, per the chief's order," Bud explained, his face turning red.

"I don't believe you." Josh's voice dipped to a lethal level. "The chief would have told us if he had you in play." Josh reached for Bud's arm. "Get up!"

A surreal numbness tore through Serena.

Bud was the leak.

Bile rose, burning her throat.

Her brother had respected and admired the older marshal. How could Bud betray Daniel, betray them all?

Reluctantly, Bud stood and scooted past his seatmate. Once he was in the aisle, he jerked out of Josh's grasp. He reared back, his hand curling into a fist.

"Josh!" Serena screamed a warning, but it was already too late.

Bud swung his fist, connecting with Josh's jaw.

Josh stumbled back, tripping over Felicia Simms.

Bud whirled toward her.

She released her hold on the judge and reached for her weapon.

The judge rammed his elbow into her side.

Pain exploded in her rib cage.

Bud shoved past her. She lashed out with her foot, catching him in the shin. He fell forward, trying to break his fall by grabbing on to the judge. The judge yelped, falling backward over the lap of a passenger.

Bud hauled himself upright and hustled down the aisle toward the exit.

"Oh, no, you don't!" Having righted himself, Josh lunged for Bud, wrestling him to the floor and handcuffing his hands behind his back before searching him for a weapon. A helpful flight attendant sat on Bud's legs. The passengers erupted with applause.

The judge attempted to flee.

"There's nowhere for you to go, Judge." Serena grabbed the judge by the handcuffs and jerked him back.

"Hey!" he yelped.

"Serena." Josh held something up.

She glanced back. The missing flash drive with the evidence Dylan McIntyre had collected. Surprise and disgust for Bud washed through her.

The judge groaned. "You idiot!"

"Shut up!" Bud instructed in a muffled voice. "Don't say anything."

Josh nodded his thanks to the attendant, freeing her to stand and release Bud's legs. Then Josh yanked Bud to his feet. "Come on, let's go."

Spittle flew from the judge as he yelled. "Why didn't you destroy that?"

"It's my insurance in case you turn on me," Bud spat back.

"I never should have trusted you!" the judge muttered.

"This is all your fault. We had a good thing going until you blew it with the marshal."

Serena gasped, flooded with the need to know what had happened to her brother. "Tell me about Daniel!"

"He killed him!" the judge said with glee.

Bud sputtered. "What? No, I didn't. You hit him over the head with your briefcase."

The judge shot back. "You left him to die!"

Shock siphoned the blood from Serena's brain. She met Josh's stunned gaze. The judge and Bud had just confessed to murdering her brother in front of a hundred witnesses.

"I thought you would like to know I have signed confessions from Judge Simms and Bud Hollingsworth. They both will be going to jail for a long time," Attorney General Kannon announced as he walked out of the chief's office at the Marshals Service district office. Chief Harrison and Agent Bishop filed out behind him.

Feeling as if a black burden had been lifted off her shoulders with the news, Serena pushed away from her desk, where she'd been trying to work up the gumption to write her report regarding the capture and arrest of Fred and Matilda Munders, Judge Simon Simms and the retired U.S. marshal turned traitor Bud Hollingsworth.

Across from her, sitting at his desk, Josh seemed to be struggling, too. His fingers pounded the keys on his computer so hard she expected bits of plastic to whack him in the face any moment.

He, too, rose and came around his desk to stand beside her. She felt his presence all the way to her low-heeled, stylish pumps. She'd returned to work in her power pantsuit, but for some reason the need to prove herself was decidedly lacking. Maybe the time undercover had softened her. But at the moment, she couldn't get worked up about it.

"The judge and Fred Munders apparently concocted the illegal adoption racket," Agent Bishop said. He made a face. "Though each is accusing the other of being the mastermind. Munders, however, is the man known as Mr. Big, since he was the one who brokered the deals and hired the henchmen. They are both facing charges of human trafficking, murder, assault and a whole host of other offenses, both on the federal and local level."

"As well as Hollingsworth," Chief Harrison added grimly. "Bud admitted that he'd been supplying Simms with information on the investigation in exchange for a piece of the profits. He's the one that set up the car crash and sent the thugs to the cover house. He'd traced your cell phone, Serena."

Loathing and anger filled her. Needing to hear the details of her brother's death and to understand why he was killed, she asked, "Can we speak with Bud? I have questions about Daniel."

Josh captured her hand. "Are you sure you want to put yourself through that?"

"I have to know what happened," she insisted, searching his face. "Don't you want to know?"

Josh breathed in and out, his chest rising with the motion as he seemed to consider, then slowly he nodded. "Yes, there are details I'd like filled in, too."

Serena looked at the FBI agent questioningly.

"I see no reason why not," Agent Bishop said. "I'll defer that decision to Chief Harrison."

The chief contemplated them for a moment. "I will allow it. I'd like to hear the details myself."

Nervous anticipation fluttered in Serena's stomach as they filed out of the offices and headed to the detention center. Once there, they entered a boxy room with no windows to wait for Bud to be brought in. A blue metal table sat in the center of the floor. Two chairs had been placed on one side and a single chair on the other.

The chief pulled one of the two chairs out and sat. Josh moved to a position in the corner, his arms folded over his chest, his face set in stoic silence.

Serena couldn't sit. Her nerves were jumping, her heart racing. She paced, aware of Josh's gaze tracking her movements. How could he be so calm?

This was one of the many attributes about Josh she'd grown to admire and cherish. No matter how bad things grew, he stayed in control, of himself, of the situation.

The door opened and Bud, wearing a tan jumpsuit and his hands and feet shackled by cuffs and link chain, shuffled in. Surprise flashed briefly in his eyes before shuttering to the mulish expression he'd had on the plane.

Serena stopped to glare at the man who'd taken her brother from her. Josh moved to stand beside her, his quiet support bolstering her courage to face the details of her brother's murder. A million questions flew through her mind. Why? How did Daniel end up in that alley? How had Daniel learned about the illegal baby ring?

Harrison spoke, preempting Serena's barrage. "Bud, thank you for agreeing to see us."

Bud shrugged, lowering himself to the seat across the table from his former boss. "Figure if I cooperate it'll go easier." His gaze encompassed them all. "Isn't that the line we tell the criminals we put away?"

Serena's hands fisted. Now Bud was one of those criminals. Josh's hand skimmed down her spine to settle on her lower back, the soothing gesture calming the tide of rising rage.

"Tell us about Daniel," Josh said, his voice cold.

"What's to tell?" Bud said. "He took a call that never should have allowed to happen."

"What call would that be?" Harrison asked, his deep voice low.

"Joe Delacorte. He contacted the Marshals Service. Daniel caught the call. Delacorte told Daniel that he was meeting someone named Mr. Big and was supposed to exchange his daughter for a wad of cash. But Delacorte backed out and gave Daniel all the information. Daniel planned to show up and take down Mr. Big. Somehow Simon found out what was taking place and reached out to me for damage control."

Outrage exploded through Serena. She took a step forward, wanting so badly to wipe that smug expression off Bud's face. Josh's hand slipped to her hip, his fingers pressing lightly, holding her back.

"You lured Daniel to the alleyway and killed him," Serena said between clenched teeth.

Flicking his gaze to her, Bud shook his head. Was that true regret in his eyes? "I never planned on that happening."

"You were the one he talked to while he was leaving me a message on my cell," Josh said.

Bud's lips twisted. "Yeah."

"Why didn't he inform me about the call?" Harrison asked. "He broke protocol."

Bud smirked. "I convinced him the call was a crock and that we should check the situation out before we raised a ruckus over something that could turn out to be nothing."

She could hear it now. His was the voice they'd heard on Daniel's message.

"You said Simon hit him over the head," Josh said. "Why did Simon show up if he knew Daniel would be there? To what end?"

"I was as surprised as Daniel when Simon arrived. I was expecting Munders." Bud shook his head. "Simon didn't want the scheme to go sideways, so he came up behind Daniel and hit him over the head with his briefcase before Munders arrived. Simon had it all worked out in his overinflated brain. Daniel would wake up with a headache. I'd pretend to have been hit as well and the whole thing would disappear."

"That wouldn't have worked," Josh said. "Daniel would have known something was up."

Bud shrugged.

"He was lying there on the ground bleeding, dying, and you walked away!" Serena couldn't take it anymore. She lunged at Bud.

Josh's arm snaked around her waist, restraining her, pulling her backward up against his muscled chest and propelling her out of the interrogation room.

"Let me go!" She pushed at his arms.

He released her, his hands raised as he stepped back. "Okay, sweetheart."

"Nothing will bring my brother back!" She paced away from him, her hands fisting at her sides.

"But we caught his killer."

Josh's softly spoken words wrapped around her like a tether drawing her back to him. Standing in front of him, her breaths coming in ragged waves, she let the adrenaline spike flow out of her. "You're right. We did. Together."

"And our undercover marriage is over." There was a note of finality in his tone that set off unease sliding through her. "It's time for us to get back to our real lives."

She tried to swallow past the emotion constricting her throat. It was now or never. She had to tell him how she felt before her courage deserted her. "Josh—" She stopped when a woman turned the corner and headed their way. Frustrated she grabbed Josh by the hand and tugged him down the hall toward the exit. "We need to talk, but not here. Let's go back to the cover house."

* * *

Josh followed Serena inside the house in Compton Heights. He paused in the entryway as his gaze immediately went to the place where their mock wedding portrait had hung. It was gone now. Linda had wasted no time in dismantling their equipment. Josh and Serena needed to pack up their personal belongings, and then this special operation would be behind them.

And then they would return to their separate lives. Only seeing each other on the job. Never again would he be free to take her hand, hold her close. Kiss her.

"Josh," Serena called to him.

While he'd stopped to ponder the destruction of their fake marriage, she'd continued on to the backyard. She stood on the porch, facing the beautiful yard. She'd said they needed to talk. He wasn't sure there was much to say. Despite his feelings for her, they had to reclaim the careers, the lives they'd had before being tasked with the assignment of bringing down the illegal adoption scam.

Serena faced him. Her lovely eyes were so full of emotion that his heart ached at the sight.

"I love you, Josh," she said without preamble.

Stunned joy exploded in his chest. But he quickly tamped it down. "Serena—"

She held up a hand. "I had to say it before I lost my nerve. I know I haven't been easy on you these past six months. I was wrong to be so selfish by blaming you for something that wasn't your fault. I—"

"Serena, please don't," he cut her off. "You weren't being selfish. You were being human."

She chewed on her lip.

Tenderness filled him. And he knew, deep in his soul, that nothing else mattered in this world but this wonderful, beautiful, tough and kind woman. "I can't give you up."

Her eyes widened. "You can't?"

"No. I'll have to quit the marshals and become an FBI agent."

She made a face. "What? Why?"

"Because if we're going to make a go of a real marriage, we can't work together."

Her eyes widened. Her mouth opened and closed, but nothing came out.

"In case I'm not making myself clear," he said, tugging her close. "I love you, too, Marshal Serena Summers."

Elation spread across her face. She snaked her arms around his neck. "I'm not letting you quit. We can be marshals and married."

He grimaced. "What if I break your heart? Working together would be impossible." Images of the heartbreak on his mother's face after learning of his father's treachery marched through his brain. The memory of the pain on Lexi's face when she walked out set up camp in his mind. He couldn't risk hurting Serena.

"Oh, Josh," she said, her voice full of tenderness. "You are nothing like your father. You're the most generous, steady and compassionate man I know. You were there for me when Daniel died. You've stuck by me even though I was difficult to be with. You've had my back more times than I can count. Josh, you won't break my heart. You have to have some faith. As long as we seek God's help, we can withstand anything."

He believed her. Faith would see them through. He bent his head, seeking her lips, her kiss. She met him all the way, giving of herself, her heart. His heart swelled with love and adoration for the incredible marshal in his arms.

"Hmm, now that's what I'm talking about," she murmured.

He dropped his forehead to hers. "You were wrong, you know. About Lexi."

"I was?"

"She didn't break my heart."

Serena drew back to look at his face. "No?"

"She broke up with me because she knew that I was in love with you."

A surprised and joyful smile spread across Serena's face. "Oh, really. Do tell."

He grinned. "I've been in love with you since the day Daniel introduced us. I just was too dense to realize it."

Tugging him back in for a kiss, she murmured against his lips, "Daniel would be pleased."

EPILOGUE

On the day she learned of her brother's murder, Serena had thought she'd never feel anything but sorrow and misery for the rest of her life. But as she gazed into the loving eyes of her newly wedded husband, she realized she'd been wrong. So wonderfully, thankfully, blessedly wrong.

Despite the humidity on this Fourth of July evening, she swept the train of her fitted silk column wedding gown aside and pressed closer to the tuxedoed man she loved. Her husband, friend and fellow marshal.

She couldn't get enough of him and impatiently waited to start their life together as husband and wife. Such was her nature, as he'd probably tell her. The thought made her smile. He knew her so well.

From where they sat at the place of honor reserved for the bride and groom, beneath the stars in the outdoor reception Emerson Park pavilion on the shore of Lake Owasco, she watched a brilliant display of fireworks streak across the dark night sky and thought she could imagine her brother smiling down on them. She knew in her heart he'd be happy.

Delighted contentment crowded the grief of losing her brother to the far corners of her heart. She would always miss Daniel. His death left a hole in her life. Nothing would ever heal that wound, but Josh's love soothed the hurt and stirred her soul with longing and love.

"I propose a toast." Hunter Davis, Josh's best man, stood, looking handsome in his tux, and raised his glass of sparkling apple cider, served in honor of his pregnant wife, Annie.

Annie, dressed in a pretty pink dress, which set off her rosy cheeks, sat next to Hunter, glowing with an inner bliss that couldn't be missed. On her lap sat her daughter Sophia, playing with a doll.

"To the bride and groom," Hunter said. "Josh, Serena, may your years together be happy, healthy and full of love and faith in God, who gives us abundant blessings."

Hunter's gaze moved to his wife and softened to adoration. They had made the decision to return to St. Louis for the event, but intended to go back to their new Montana home, where they had several acres of land and room for their children to grow. Josh understood, but Serena knew he missed his friend.

"To the happy couple," Chief Harrison's voice boomed. He'd brought his lovely wife. Serena had liked her instantly.

"Here, here," Colton Phillips called out, lifting his glass. Sitting to Colton's left, FBI special agent Lisette Sutton beamed. They'd flown in from Denver to attend the nuptials. They were engaged, their wedding date set for after the New Year. Josh and Serena were already planning their trip west for the event.

"To the newlyweds!" Burke Trier shouted. He'd brought a date with him tonight. When they'd arrived, he'd whispered to Serena that he thought this one might be "the one." The day Burke settled down would be a banner day.

More cheers and good wishes were uttered from the small, intimate group of friends and relatives. Serena's gaze swept over those gathered. Love and gratitude flooded her.

Josh's mom and grandparents had come from Florida. Serena's parents had shown up as well, but sat at separate tables from each other. Par for the course.

Linda Maitland sat with Eve Cardinalli and Lonnie Bogler. Eve and Lonnie had declined going into witness protection. Eve had said what good was faith if she didn't believe God would protect her.

Emma Bullock and Officer Zach Jones were at that table, as well. The couple had been visiting Eve and Lonnie often this past month as they worked with Linda tracking down the babies and mothers separated by everyone involved in Perfect Family Adoption's despicable actions.

Serena heard Zach tell Josh he was planning to propose to Emma this week. Giddy anticipation for Emma's happiness raced through Serena. She wanted everyone to be as full of joy as she was.

Little Crystal Kay toddled around the tables, looking adorable in a frilly dress and shiny shoes. Watching her filled Serena with a deep yearning that was getting harder to resist. She wondered how soon was too soon to start a family. Hmm, something to discuss with her husband. Elation bubbled up and she giggled. She liked calling Josh her husband.

Off to the side was a table laden with gifts. Serena had poked through them, feeling like a kid at Christmas, anxious to unwrap the presents. Her heart had swelled with love and gratitude as she recognized the WitSec names given to Dylan and Grace McIntyre, and Morgan and Alex Reardon, and Hunter and Annie Davis.

In the days following the arrests and arraignments of the Munderses, the Simms brothers, Bud and all the henchmen they could round up, Serena and Josh had made trips. One to Hawaii, where the McIntyre family now resided, content in paradise. And one to the Seattle area where the Reardons had been relocated to. Morgan and Alex had started a home for at-risk youth.

Needless to say they were all elated and thankful to hear of the arrests and looked forward to testifying at the trials. But to be safe, each family had elected to stay within the program.

Serena clinked her glass to Josh's. "I love you," she said.

"I love you, too. And I'll always be there for you."

"You won't always have to be, Josh. Because God will be there for both of us."

He laughed. "Now that's what I call backup."

* * * * *

Dear Reader,

I hope you enjoyed the ending to the Witness Protection continuity starring the men and women of the U.S. Marshals Service and the important work they do. I hope you'll forgive the liberties taken for the sake of the series.

Writing a continuity is always challenging, keeping track of all the moving pieces and plot lines and making sure to tie up any loose threads of story by the end. Since U.S. marshals Josh McCall and Serena Summers appeared in each book of the series, I was happy to let them have their own story. Helping these two resolve their conflicts and solve the mystery of who killed Marshal Daniel Summers, as well as take down the masterminds behind the illegal adoption ring so that Josh and Serena could have their very own happy ending, was satisfying. I hope you agree.

I'm starting a new series of my own showcasing the men and women who protect our northern border. I'll be posting titles and release dates as I have them on my website, www.terrireed.com.

Until we meet again, may God bless you richly.

Questions for Discussion

1. What made you pick up this book to read? In what ways did it live up to your expectations?

2. In what ways were Josh and Serena realistic characters? How did their romance build believably?

3. What about the setting was clear and appealing? Could you "see" where the story took place?

4. Serena's brother had been her anchor, especially growing up. Do you have someone in your life who has played a significant role? In what way?

5. Serena's brother was murdered. In her grief, she blamed Josh. Can you talk about the reasons she did and why this was or was not warranted?

6. Josh felt guilty for Daniel's death. In what ways was he or was he not responsible?

7. Is forgiving oneself easier or harder than forgiving someone else?

8. During Josh's childhood his father went to prison. This traumatic event shaped the rest of his life. Can you talk about an event you've experienced that changed your life?

9. Do you believe that circumstances shouldn't dictate our faith? Can you share a time when you let the circumstances of your life influence your faith?

10. Were the secondary characters believable? Did they add to the story? In what way?

11. Going undercover as a married couple forced Josh and Serena to find a way to be unified. Unity in marriage takes work. Can you discuss the conflicts they had to overcome and the issues they had to face? What conflicts or issues have you had to face in your marriage or significant relationship? How have these challenges helped you move toward unity?

12. Did you notice the scripture in the beginning of the book? What do you think God means by these words? What application does the scripture have to your life?

13. How did the author's use of language/writing style make this an enjoyable read?

14. Would you read more from this author? If so, why? Or why not?

15. What will be your most vivid memories of this book? Of the whole series?

COMING NEXT MONTH FROM
Love Inspired® Suspense

Available July 1, 2014

PROTECTIVE INSTINCTS
Mission: Rescue • by Shirlee McCoy

Someone is stalking widow Raina Lowery. But she has no idea who or why. As the threats escalate for her and her foster son, former marine Jackson Miller must do his best to protect Raina from the past—and create a safe new future together.

SHAKE DOWN • by Jill Elizabeth Nelson
To Janice Swenson, the Martha's Vineyard cottage is an unwanted inheritance. Yet to Shane Gillum, it's the hiding spot for evidence to clear his father's name. But as he searches for answers, he finds danger that puts their lives at risk.

FLOOD ZONE
Stormswept • by Dana Mentink

Dallas Black has to find a way to protect Mia Sandoval and her young daughter from a killer on the loose and the perilous floodwaters that threaten the town.

CRITICAL DIAGNOSIS • by Alison Stone
When army physician James O'Reilly returns to his hometown, he finds himself protecting pretty researcher Lily McAllister from a ruthless stalker on her trail.

CAUGHT IN THE CROSSHAIRS • by Elisabeth Rees
When their simple mission goes horribly wrong, military sniper Cara Hanson and Captain Dean McGovern go into hiding and must work together to find the true culprit.

SMOKY MOUNTAIN INVESTIGATION
by Annslee Urban

Reporting on a serial killer turns terrifying when journalist Kylie Harper becomes his new target. Now ex-boyfriend Nick Bentley must risk his life and his heart to keep Kylie safe.

REQUEST YOUR FREE BOOKS!
2 FREE RIVETING INSPIRATIONAL NOVELS
PLUS 2 FREE MYSTERY GIFTS

YES! Please send me 2 FREE Love Inspired® Suspense novels and my 2 FREE mystery gifts (gifts are worth about $10). After receiving them, if I don't wish to receive any more books, I can return the shipping statement marked "cancel." If I don't cancel, I will receive 4 brand-new novels every month and be billed just $4.74 per book in the U.S. or $5.24 per book in Canada. That's a savings of at least 21% off the cover price. It's quite a bargain! Shipping and handling is just 50¢ per book in the U.S. and 75¢ per book in Canada.* I understand that accepting the 2 free books and gifts places me under no obligation to buy anything. I can always return a shipment and cancel at any time. Even if I never buy another book, the two free books and gifts are mine to keep forever.

123/323 IDN F5AC

Name _____ (PLEASE PRINT) _____

Address _____ Apt. # _____

City _____ State/Prov. _____ Zip/Postal Code _____

Signature (if under 18, a parent or guardian must sign)

Mail to the **Harlequin® Reader Service:**
IN U.S.A.: P.O. Box 1867, Buffalo, NY 14240-1867
IN CANADA: P.O. Box 609, Fort Erie, Ontario L2A 5X3

Are you a current subscriber to Love Inspired Suspense books and want to receive the larger-print edition?
Call 1-800-873-8635 or visit www.ReaderService.com.

* Terms and prices subject to change without notice. Prices do not include applicable taxes. Sales tax applicable in N.Y. Canadian residents will be charged applicable taxes. Offer not valid in Quebec. This offer is limited to one order per household. Not valid for current subscribers to Love Inspired Suspense books. All orders subject to credit approval. Credit or debit balances in a customer's account(s) may be offset by any other outstanding balance owed by or to the customer. Please allow 4 to 6 weeks for delivery. Offer available while quantities last.

Your Privacy—The Harlequin® Reader Service is committed to protecting your privacy. Our Privacy Policy is available online at www.ReaderService.com or upon request from the Harlequin Reader Service.

We make a portion of our mailing list available to reputable third parties that offer products we believe may interest you. If you prefer that we not exchange your name with third parties, or if you wish to clarify or modify your communication preferences, please visit us at www.ReaderService.com/consumerchoice or write to us at Harlequin Reader Service Preference Service, P.O. Box 9062, Buffalo, NY 14269. Include your complete name and address.

LIS13R

SPECIAL EXCERPT FROM

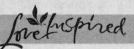

*Join the ranching town of Jasper Gulch, Montana,
as they celebrate 100 years!*

**Here's a sneak peek at
HER MONTANA COWBOY
by Valerie Hansen, the first of six books in the
BIG SKY CENTENNIAL miniseries.**

For the first time in longer than Ryan Travers could recall, he was having trouble keeping his mind on his work. He couldn't have cared less about Jasper Gulch's missing time capsule; it was pretty Julie Shaw who occupied his thoughts.

"That's not good," he muttered as he stood on a metal rung of the narrow bucking chute. This rangy pinto mare wasn't called Widow-maker for nothing. He could not only picture Julie Shaw as if she were standing right there next to the chute gates, he could imagine her light, uplifting laughter.

Actually, he realized with a start, that *was* what he was hearing. He started to glance over his shoulder, intending to scan the nearby crowd and, hopefully, locate her.

"Clock's ticking, Travers," the chute boss grumbled. "You gonna ride that horse or just look at her?"

Rather than answer with words, Ryan stepped across the top of the chute, raised his free hand over his head and leaned way back. Then he nodded to the gateman.

The latch clicked.

The mare leaped.

Ryan didn't attempt to do anything but ride until he heard the horn blast announcing his success. Then he straightened as best he could and worked his fingers loose with his free hand while pickup men maneuvered close enough to help him dismount.

To Ryan's delight, Julie Shaw and a few others he recognized from before were watching. They had parked a flatbed farm truck near the fence beside the grandstand and were watching from secure perches in its bed.

Julie had both arms raised and was still cheering so wildly she almost knocked her hat off. "Woo-hoo! Good ride, cowboy!"

Ryan's "Thanks" was swallowed up in the overall din from the rodeo fans. Clearly, Julie wasn't the only spectator who had been favorably impressed.

He knew he should immediately report to the area behind the strip chutes and pick up his rigging. And he would. In a few minutes. As soon as he'd spoken to his newest fan.

Don't miss the romance between Julie and rodeo hero Ryan in HER MONTANA COWBOY by Valerie Hansen, available July 2014 from Love Inspired®.

"Who would want to hurt you, Raina?" Jackson asked her.

"No one," she replied, her mind working frantically, going
through faces and names and situations.

"And yet, someone chased you through the woods. That
same person nearly ran me down. Doesn't sound like someone
who feels all warm and fuzzy when he thinks of you."

"Maybe he was a vagrant, and I scared him."

"Maybe." He didn't sound like he believed it, and she
wasn't sure she did, either.

She'd heard something that had woken her from the
nightmare.

A child crying? Her neighbor Larry wandering around?
An intruder trying to get into the house?

The last thought made her shudder, and she pulled her coat
a little closer. "I think I'd know it if someone had a bone to
pick with me."

"That's usually the case, but not always. Could be you
upset a coworker, said no to a guy who wanted you to say
yes—"

She snorted at that, and Jackson frowned. "You've been a widow for four years. It's not that far-fetched an idea."

"If you got a good look at my social life you wouldn't be saying that."

Samuel yawned loudly and slid down on the pew, his arms crossed over his chest, his eyelids drooping. The ten-year-old looked cold and tired, and she wanted to get him home and tuck him into bed.

"I'll go talk to Officer Wallace," Jackson responded. "See if he's ready to let us leave."

"He's going to have to be. Samuel—"

A door slammed, the sound so startling Raina jumped.

She grabbed Samuel's shoulder, pulled him into the shelter of her arms.

"Is someone else in the church?" Jackson demanded, his gaze on the door that led from the sanctuary into the office wing.

"There shouldn't be."

"Stay put. I'm going to check things out."

He strode away, and she wanted to call out and tell him to be careful.

She pressed her lips together, held in the words she knew she didn't need to say. She'd seen him in action, knew just how smart and careful he was.

Jackson could take care of himself.

*Will Jackson discover the stalker and help
Raina find a second chance at love?*

*Pick up PROTECTIVE INSTINCTS to find out.
Available July 2014 wherever
Love Inspired® Suspense books are sold.*

LISEXP0614